CYNTHIA HICKEY

MISTAKEN ASSASSIN
Overcoming Evil, Book 1
By Cynthia Hickey

Copyright © **2013**
Written by: Cynthia Hickey
Published by: Winged Publications
Cover Design: Cynthia Hickey

- **ISBN-10:** 1495323145
- **ISBN-13:** 978-1495323140

CHAPTER ONE

Marilu Hutchins opened her eyes and stared at the man in bed next to her. He wasn't her husband. Her husband was, or used to be, Jack Hutchins. He'd been her world...and she'd killed him.

Her heart thudded, pounding out a heavy metal beat in her ears. Without moving her head, she glanced out of the corner of her eyes at the man sleeping beside her. She willed her heart rate to slow, her breathing to quiet.

With the force of a tornado, Mari's memory returned, along with the horror of watching her husband gunned down. She again felt the bullets rip through her flesh. She heard her cries as she reached for Jack, then darkness as her head had collided with the rock.

Tears welled and flowed, soaking the pillow beneath her head. They'd had a child. A little girl. Was she with Mari's parents? Were they still living in the small Ozark town Mari had grown up in?

Placing her palms flat on the mattress, she pushed herself slowly to a sitting position and slid her legs over the side of the bed. A low snort from the man beside her caused her to freeze, until his snoring resumed. What would he do, this John Hoover as she knew him, if he discovered her memory had returned? Surely he knew she wasn't really Stacy Hoover. Right? He couldn't be innocent in this game of deceit, could he?

Without turning on the bedroom light, she felt her way to the bathroom. Her fingers trailed over the cool walls. She trod over the plush fibers of the carpet. After closing the door, she stuffed a towel under the door and locked it before switching on the light. Her eyes widened as she caught a glimpse of herself in the mirror.

A stranger stared back. One with light crow's feet spreading away from deep blue eyes that her Jack had said he could drown in. A short razor cut had her blonde hair framing cheeks which had lost their youthful roundness.

Mari frowned. She racked her brain for details. Details of her past. How long had she been lost? Ten years? Eleven? Her baby would be twelve…if she were still alive. She shook her head. What had caused these apparent memories to return?

"Stacy?" A knock on the door caused her to whirl around. She covered her mouth to stifle the scream igniting in her throat. She despised this sign of fear that came with surprise. "Are you all right?"

"I'm fine … John. I'm sorry I woke you." Mari took a deep breath to calm herself.

"Let me in." The door handle rattled.

She kicked the towel away and unlocked the door, stepping back as it swung open. John's brown eyes squinted beneath his mussed dark hair. "Are you all right? Are you sick?"

Concern etched his features and nausea rose in Mari's stomach at the man's award-winning act. Well, she'd been trained to act, too. "I'm feeling sick to my stomach." She turned away and planted her hands against the sink. "Go back to bed. I'll be there in a minute. It's only female problems. Nothing to worry about."

It took every ounce of will power she possessed not to jerk away when he placed his hands on her. Strong hands kneaded the knots in her shoulders.

"You sure you don't want me to sit with you?"

She shook her head. "You've got work tomorrow. I'll be fine. Really." She turned back to him and forced her lips into the semblance of a smile.

He frowned. His head tilted to one side as he studied her. "Okay, honey." He stepped forward and planted a kiss on her forehead. "Try to get some rest. I'm not the only one who's got work in a few hours."

Mari forced her gaze to meet his. "Sure. I'll be there soon."

Her knees buckled, threatening to give way as he turned and left, pulling the door closed behind him. Sobs rose in her throat, and she choked them back. She lunged for the toilet, losing the contents of her stomach before sliding to the floor.

Ten years. Gone. Lost in the recesses of her tormented mind while she'd played at being wife to a stranger. She searched her brain for what could have triggered the return of her memory.

They'd stayed home last night. Rented a movie. An older release. About an international spy. An assassin whose memory had returned and rocked her world. The movie had made her uncomfortable. Fidgety. Now she knew why. She'd been the same as the main character … once upon a time.

The memories continued to bombard her, and she felt herself hurled through space, back to that fateful time when she'd killed her husband as surely as if she'd pulled the trigger herself.

They'd left Jeanna with Mari's parents and taken a picnic lunch to the mountains. Mari had important news to tell her husband, Jack. News she wasn't sure how he'd react to once he'd heard.

They were an assassination team. The two of them.

3

Guns for hire. Living well off the money they earned. Then, Mari had failed an assignment. Her first assignment. She found herself unable to pull the trigger on the minister within her sights. She didn't know why the man of God was a target, only that she'd accepted the assignment. Instead, she'd found herself listening to the message he practiced as he paced the floor of his office. Her heart constricted. She'd lowered her weapon, sliding to the floor, the wall against her back. It was because of the man's words of love and forgiveness that she'd accepted Christ that day. She'd planned on telling Jack during their picnic.

She'd hand-fed him as they giggled like two love-struck teenagers. Then she'd dropped the bombshell on him. Mari knew he'd be angry, but foreknowledge didn't prepare her for his reaction. He'd erupted in anger. Screamed that she'd killed them both. His steel gray eyes had focused on her in cold fury, freezing her heart. He grabbed both her arms and shook her, rattling her teeth. Then the shots had rung out.

Jack spun around in a macabre dance as three bullets slammed into him. Two more drove through Mari, throwing her to the ground. She'd seen the rock in that split second before her head connected with it.

That's all she remembered. Not how she got out of that place or how she'd ended up with John Hoover. She suspected he was her guardian. A man put in place to find out what she remembered, when, and if she ever did. But what was it they wanted her to show them? What were they afraid of her knowing? Why not kill her and leave her body beside that of her husband?

She'd stalled enough. Mari pushed to her feet and stumbled to the sink. She filled her cupped hands under the faucet and rinsed the sour taste from her mouth. Turning to the door, she eased it open. John would be leaving for work in a few hours, and Mari had plans to make.

The door squeaked as she swung it open. She halted, catching her breath at the sight of John sitting on the edge of the bed.

"Feel better?" His hard voice caused her limbs to tremble.

"I threw up."

"That's too bad." He patted the mattress beside him. "Join me, Stacy."

She scooted her feet across the carpet. "I'll sit in the easy chair. I'm sure I'll be up again. I don't want to keep you awake." Her body tensed, poised for flight.

"Well." He clenched his fist and rolled his head around on his neck. "It was bound to happen sooner or later. How much do you remember?"

His words stopped her midway to sitting on the chair. Her rump suspended over the cushion as she balanced her hands on the arms of the chair. "What?"

He stood and began to pace. "Don't play stupid with me, *Marilu*. How much do you remember?"

"Remember what? John, you're scaring me. Who's Marilu?" Mari rose and paced opposite him, the two circling each other like wrestlers in a ring. She thanked God for the fact she'd slept in flannel pants and a tee shirt instead of a nightgown.

John held his hands loose at his side. "Darling. Why are you afraid of me? We've shared ten years together." He lunged toward her and she jumped to the side.

"Ten years of a lie. Who are you?"

"I'm John Hoover." He skipped toward her, reaching for her arm. His fingers brushed across her skin. "So you do remember something."

"A little. I know my name isn't Stacy Hoover." Mari's own fists clenched. "Why am I still alive? Why have you kept me here for so long?"

"Would you rather we had left you beside your dead husband?"

"Yes." Tears welled in Mari's eyes. "So he *is* dead." It wasn't a nightmare.

John shrugged. "Personally, I didn't check. We'd left you for dead, too, but found you wandering the countryside the next day. Jack's body was gone. Maybe the animals got him. Maybe he's alive and crazy somewhere, too." His lips thinned into a sneer. "You were loonier than a bat; had no idea who, or where, you were. But if we do find him, we'll finish what we started all those years ago."

Hope rose in Mari's chest only to be quenched. If Jack were alive, he'd have looked for her, wouldn't he? "Why the pretending? Why you?"

"It's the best way to keep an eye on someone, being married to them. Why not me? You're a looker. It wasn't a hardship. I've even come to care for you … a little." He lunged again, managing to dart behind her. His arm circled her throat, and he squeezed. "I need to know that you'll cooperate."

Spots danced before her eyes as the pressure increased. She kicked her feet, aiming for his shins.

John cursed and lifted her off her feet. "Time to get some sleep, love." He lifted her limp body in his arms and deposited her on the bed. Mari's breath wheezed through her throat as he stepped back.

He disappeared from her sight, only to return grasping a syringe. "Here's something to help you get that rest you so desperately need."

Digging deep inside herself, Mari grabbed hold of the strength born from years of rigorous workouts and rolled from the bed. She hit the floor with a thump and gasped, feeling like a stranded fish. Struggling to draw air through her tortured throat, she leaped to her feet.

John's eyes shone with anticipation as his mouth curved into a sneer. "Okay. The lady wants to dance. Do you think you remember how?"

Clouded visions of martial arts and bodily contact flitted through Mari's mind. "Oh, I think so." If she remembered correctly, she'd been a lethal weapon, her hands and feet striking with lightning precision and speed. She prayed she hadn't lost it all.

John started to move to her side of the bed, and she rolled across the mattress. She landed on her feet on the other side. Her eyes remained glued to the man across from her.

He laughed. The sound sent shivers of dread down her spine. Again she prayed to the God she'd once known. Prayed He hadn't forgotten her. Prayed she would remember her skills.

CHAPTER TWO

J ohn feinted to one side in an attempt to confuse Mari and she braced herself, not taking the bait. He laughed again and lunged across the bed. Mari dove, crash-landing on the floor. The impact drove the air from her lungs again. John landed on top of her. The scent of carpet freshener wafted up her nostrils, and she sneezed.

Holding one arm around her throat, John pushed to his feet. He pulled Mari with him. In a rush, her defensive training returned to her. She raised her leg behind her in a rear lift kick to John's groin. Quickly turning, she drove her elbow into his face with enough force she felt his nose break. Blood spurted across her as he collapsed to the floor. A Shuto chop to the man's neck rendered him unconscious, and Mari stood over him, her chest heaving.

The ease of her violent retaliation left her stunned. Numb. She'd fought as if she'd been doing so for years, while in reality, the last ten had been years of relative calm, even boredom, as she'd kept his house. She'd been content in her role as housewife and part-time secretary. Her only physical exercise had been a few nights at the local gym. Nausea rose and she swallowed it down, the acid burning her esophagus.

She had to leave.

Now.

Mari knelt beside the nightstand and rummaged through it until she located John's wallet. She pulled cash from the leather billfold and stuffed the bills into her purse, not taking the time to count them. She then withdrew the pistol John kept beside the bed and shoved it into the bottom of her handbag.

John groaned, spurring her faster. She darted across the room and yanked open the closet door. From the top shelf, she pulled down a small suitcase and tossed random items inside. Sweatshirts, jeans, gym shoes, underwear. Her gaze fell on the steel box in the corner.

The safe.

Heart beating out a quick tempo, almost drowning out the groans emanating through John's lips, Mari knelt. Her fingers flew across the keypad lock. Several wrapped bundles of bills laid stacked inside, and she tossed these inside the suitcase, then snapped it closed.

Suitcase in hand, she slung her purse over her shoulder and rummaged with her free hand for her keys. As she ran past John, he groaned and rolled over, face pressing into the pool of blood draining from his shattered nose.

His hands cupped his groin. "Marilu, they'll kill you." His voice sounded distorted.

Her blood chilled at his garbled words. She knew he spoke the truth and prayed for God to protect her.

Bare feet slapped against wood paneled floors as Mari raced from the bedroom, down the hall, across the living room, into the kitchen, and out to the garage. Her silver Lexus sat beside John's massive SUV. She grabbed a screwdriver from a nearby shelf and plunged it into the SUV's tires. One by one, she stabbed at them, forcing the tool through the thick rubber before tossing it back on the workbench.

Behind the wheel of her car, she pressed the button for the garage door. She waited, afraid to breathe. Her gaze remained locked on the door leading into the house, expecting John to appear at any second. After what seemed an eternity, the door completed its slow climb. She threw the car in reverse and roared from the driveway.

She glanced in the rearview mirror. John stood hunkered in the middle of the road. A gun held loosely in his hand. He aimed. The shot went wild. Mari pressed the accelerator. Soon, John was nothing but a speck in the distance.

She trembled as the adrenaline rush wore off, replaced by confusion. She'd fought as the trained killer she'd once been. Would she still be able to kill if the need arose or had God taken that trait from her? She prayed He had, at the same time she hoped He hadn't.

The past washed over her so quickly, it threatened to drown out the previous ten years, becoming more real than her life with John. The false life, she now called it. She tightened her grip in an effort to still the trembling. Her knuckles turned white with the strain.

"Where do I go?" Her voice sounded hoarse. The words pushed past her bruised throat. "I want to see my daughter."

To go back to her parent's home would be foolish. She might as well lead her pursuers to their door and put the gun in their hands. An icy steeliness ran down her spine. She'd protect her child and parents at all costs. Even if it meant she'd never lay eyes on Jeanna again.

A light drizzle began to fall, casting the early dawn light in shimmers of liquid color. Marilu glanced at the rearview mirror. How long until they followed her?

She'd have to ditch the car. Find something more ordinary. She swerved the Lexus into an all-night supermarket. There was little to choose from, this early in the morning. Her gaze fell on a white Toyota Corolla of an old enough model, she wouldn't have difficulty hot-wiring it. She drove the Lexus behind the store and parked.

Please let the car be unlocked. Please let the car be unlocked. Mari grabbed the vehicle registration papers from the glove compartment, then snatched her suitcase and purse before sprinting to the waiting Corolla. She tried the door handle. Locked. She turned, searching the nearby ground for something to break the window. A rock. Grabbing a fist-sized stone, Mari bashed the window and let the rock fall to the ground.

A spider-web spread across the busted window, and she thrust her elbow through, sending diamonds of shattered glass to the vinyl seats. Sharp pain burst through her arm, and she squelched down a scream.

The rain fell harder, plastering her hair to her head and obscuring her vision. Distant sirens pierced the air, and her heart stuttered.

She jerked the door open. It slammed against her shin. Sharp stabs of pain radiated down her leg. *Settle down. Crippling yourself won't help anything.* She slid onto the vinyl seats, unmindful of the glass, and tossed her suitcase in the back.

Taking a moment she could ill afford to spend, she stared at the dashboard and steering column. How could she get to the wires? The rock. She leaned from the car and retrieved the rock she'd dropped. With two hard bashes to the dashboard, she exposed the wires, then tossed the rock to the passenger side floorboard.

Removing the ends from the colored wires, she touched the black and red wires together. She laughed out loud when the car started, and she slammed the door closed. Despite the increasing rain being driven through the shattered window, her spirits lifted. She pressed her foot to the pedal and sped from the parking lot. As soon as she got somewhere safe, she'd mail cash to the address on the papers in the glove compartment.

As she drove, she dug through her purse for her weapon

and laid it on the seat within easy reach. *Please, God, don't let me have to use it.* She chastised herself, knowing eventually she'd face the need to kill or be killed. What she might have to do frightened her.

Headlights appeared behind her, and Mari held her breath until the truck sped past, spraying the car with dirty water from the street. Some of the spray washed through the car's window, and she groaned. She lifted her tee-shirt to dry her face, then remembered John's blood spattered across it and stopped. Instead, she wiped her face on her equally wet forearm.

She glanced in the rearview mirror. A hard, wet, red-streaked face stared back. A face that wasn't unfamiliar. She'd been covered with blood before. A slideshow of images flashed through her mind. Faces of strangers. Eyes glazed over with death. *God, what kind of a monster was I?*

She knew the answer to that question. She'd been a woman who was trained to kill without remorse. One interested only in the cash earned from the killing. Caring only for her husband, child, and parents. Her heart constricted at the thought. How was that possible? How could she love a handful of people so deeply, and think others weren't worthy of life? Had her heart been that hard before Christ entered?

Headlights pulled up close behind her, and she caught her breath in alarm. Had they found her so soon? She accelerated. The vehicle behind her did the same. More acceleration and the steering wheel vibrated beneath her hands. She fought to keep the car steady on the rain-slick road.

The blare of a horn hit her ears, and the truck sped past her. Three young men hooted and yelled. One hung out the passenger side window, oblivious to the rain, and hurled a beer bottle at the Corolla. It bounced off the windshield and the man laughed, sending Mari an obscene gesture.

She squelched the desire to speed after them and put a

bullet in their tires, instead taking deep breaths to steady her heart. She released her foot a bit on the accelerator.

Ahead, the sun peeked over the horizon, shining gold and orange in the sky. The rain had slowed to a drizzle. Mari breathed deeply of the fresh morning air blowing through the broken window. She glanced again in the mirror. Her heart stilled at the flashing red and blue lights from the police cruiser behind her.

CHAPTER THREE

Her heart seemed to stop beating, then burst into a rapid Salsa dance as the cruiser sped past and disappeared across the horizon. Mari withdrew her hand that had covered the handgun in a reflex action. She released her breath in a painful whoosh.

The recent events of the day left her exhausted. She scanned the roads leading away from the highway. The need for sleep became a top priority.

Beaten down weeds signaled a little used road to her right, and she sent the little car fishtailing on the wet asphalt as she yanked the steering wheel. Pebbles and small rocks bounced, hitting the Corolla's undercarriage as she jostled down a poor excuse for a road. Tree branches scratched the sides of the car like fingers down a chalkboard.

Deciding she'd gone far enough to be hidden from the highway, she cut the engine and let her head fall back against the seat. What was she going to do now?

She turned her head and peered into the foliage. The trees and brush grew so thick they cut out the early morning light, leaving her in a semi-gloom. The rain beat a gentle rhythm against the car's roof. Her eyelids grew heavy, and closed.

A snuffling sound in her left ear woke her. A small yelp escaped her, and she reached for her weapon. She opened her eyes to stare into a very large pair of brown orbs.

The cow stretched its wet nose toward Mari's face. Giggling, she shoved the cow's head back out the window. "Go on, you big brute." She swivelled her head, searching for signs of a nearby farm.

She brought her gaze back to the brown and white animal who continued to regard her with curiosity. "Where did you come from, girl?"

Mari opened the door and squeezed past the animal blocking her way. Pressing her hands on the small of her back, she leaned backward until her vertebra popped with a satisfying snap. She straightened and listened. No sounds of home life reached her ears. Just those of the woods. Birds and insects twittered and buzzed from the surrounding foliage.

"Are you lost, you big beauty?" She reached over and ran a hand down the silky softness of the animal's snout.

To the right, trampled grass indicated the way the animal had come, and Mari headed in that direction. Her stomach rumbled. Maybe she'd find a house where nobody was home and she could get a bite to eat.

Her mind calculated the cost of the car she'd 'borrowed'. She'd mail them the title to her Lexus in trade. She didn't want to add theft to her ever-growing list of sins. If she took someone's food, she'd leave cash. She headed back to the car and grabbed her purse after stuffing the gun inside and transferring the money from the suitcase. If she didn't make it back to the car, she wouldn't leave the cash for someone else to take.

Fifteen minutes later, Mari watched from behind a tree as an elderly woman pinned clothes to a clothesline. She assessed the area. Several cows grazed in a field nearby. A barn peppered with woodpecker holes sat between the small clapboard house and the field. A gravel drive passed behind the sea-foam green house.

Her stomach protested again. Suddenly the cow nosed her in the shoulder, sending her off balance and stumbling into the yard. She landed on her hands and knees in the grass. She lifted her head to stare into the astonished eyes of the woman hanging clothes.

"Land sakes, child!" The woman dropped the shirt she held and bustled to Mari's side. "You found Claire. The cantankerous old thing is always getting out. I hope she didn't hurt you none."

"No, I'm all right. Thank you."

The woman glanced at her tee shirt. Mari wished she'd had a chance to change clothes before running into someone.

"What happened to you, child?"

Lord, forgive me. "I'm prone to nosebleeds." Mari tossed her chin in the direction she came. "I had a little car trouble back a ways. It's fixed now, but I was wondering whether I could trouble you for a drink?"

"You sure can. Let me get this cow put away. Why don't you have a seat on the porch there? I won't be but a minute."

Mari crossed the grass and sank gratefully on the top wooden step. She watched as the woman led the brown and white cow to where the other bovines grazed. The clearing the house sat in was peaceful, and she took a deep breath. The air smelled of fresh mowed grass.

"I'm Agnes," the woman said through a smile as she climbed the stairs. She wadded her flowered house dress above chubby knees. "Who are you?"

"Mary." Mari rose. "I'm so grateful. If I could get a drink of water, I'll be on my way."

Agnes pushed open the screen door. "I've the makings of a sandwich sitting out. Ham and Swiss. Let me make you one. You can take it with you, or stay and chat. I'd like the company." She waved Mari ahead of her into a large country kitchen with a small wooden table in the center of the room.

A blackened potbelly stove sat in a corner of the room. No fire burned in its depths. In another corner stood a gaggle of wooden geese, adding country charm to the room. Robin's egg blue cabinets ran along one wall.

"I really don't want to trouble you. A glass of water would be fine." Mari's stomach growled in protest.

Agnes laughed. "I heard that from here. Sit down, Mary. Let me fix you that sandwich." She opened the refrigerator and withdrew a glass pitcher of lemonade. "This'll take care of your thirst. Squeezed it just this morning." She poured a tall glass, added ice, and then set it on the table.

Mari's mouth watered at the sight, and she reached eagerly for the offered glass. She closed her eyes, savoring the lemony sweet taste of heaven as it slid down her throat. Within minutes, she held a thick ham sandwich.

"Do you live out here alone?" she asked before taking a bite.

Agnes pulled up a chair across from her, a sandwich in her hand. "No. My husband Carl's out fixing the hole in the fence Claire escaped through." The woman's blue eyes focused on Mari's face. She set her sandwich on a napkin. "Honey, I know that blood on your shirt didn't come from your nose. You've got bruises across your neck, and you look like you've been to the bad place and back." She raised a hand against Mari's protest. "You ain't the first abused woman I've seen, and I doubt you'll be the last." She leaned across the table. "You got a place to go?"

Did she? Mari had no idea, but she decided to let the woman believe the abuse story. She hadn't thought farther than the next day and a quick stop at a drugstore for hair color. "I'm headed home to my parents."

Agnes patted her hand. "That's good. That's real good."

The sandwich tasted like ambrosia, and for the first time that day, Mari glanced at her watch. She'd napped for two hours. The next thing on the agenda was to find a hotel far enough away from John's house so she could get a good night's sleep.

"You got enough money, Mary?"

The kindness in the woman's eyes was almost her undoing. Guilt caused a lump to lodge in her throat at her continuing deception. She swallowed again and lowered her eyes to the table in front of her.

She brushed the sandwich crumbs from the yellow and white checkered tablecloth into her hand, grateful the task gave her something to do besides let the tears in her eyes fall.

Mari rummaged in her purse and pulled out a twenty dollar bill. "Please. Take this for your kindness." She held the money out to the old woman.

Agnes frowned, her brows meeting above her pained eyes. "I can't take your money for doing what the good Lord would have me do. Put it away before you hurt my feelings."

"I'm sorry. It's just that I'm…" Mari's gut clenched as she stared out the window behind the older woman's head. A dark blue truck crunched down the driveway followed by a black SUV.

CHAPTER FOUR

Mari rose rigidly from her chair. The half-eaten sandwich fell to the table.

"What is it, dear?" Agnes moved to peer out the window. "Is that your husband?"

"Yes."

A clean, smiling John, wearing freshly pressed pants stepped from the SUV and shook hands with Agnes's husband. The older man glanced toward the house.

"I've got to leave. I need to go *now*." Mari snatched her purse from where she'd hung it on the back of the chair. She tossed a glance over her shoulder. John sprinted toward the house.

"Mary…" Agnes stretched a hand in her direction.

Mari raced through the small house, bursting out the front door like a champagne cork. She darted across the yard, hoping to seek refuge in the woods.

"Stacy!" John sprinted around the corner of the house. His tackle drove Mari to the ground. Her purse flew to the ground as her shoulder connected with a small rock. The handle of her weapon taunted her from within the brown leather. She cried out as the pain turned to numbness.

"Sweetheart? Do you promise to behave if I let you up?" His words were soft in her ear, yet she knew they carried to the couple standing on the porch. The words contrasted with the pinch he gave her tender underarm.

His words softened to a whisper. "Get up nice and easy or I kill the old folks. Understand? Not a word out of your mouth."

She nodded, tears welling in her eyes. Her fist closed around the rock she'd fallen on. Its solidness gave her confidence. As John yanked her to her feet, she slipped the rock into the pocket of her sweatpants.

Keeping a firm grip on her elbow, John tugged her back toward the house. He bent and grasped the purse as they walked by. Mari swallowed against her rising fear as the handgun vanished within the recesses of the purse.

"How'd you find me?" she hissed.

"Wasn't hard. I just checked all the surrounding farms. I knew you'd stop somewhere." He turned and smiled at Agnes and her husband. "I'm very sorry about my wife's behavior. She's a bit delusional. Thinks her name is Marilu." He turned his smile to Mari. "My guess is she hasn't been taking her medication. Have you, dear?"

She kept her hand folded around the rock's hardness in her pocket. Her gaze flicked to the waiting couple, and she shook her head. Their caring, lined faces looked down at her with eyes full of compassion.

"That's okay," Agnes said, holding out a hand. "You two come on in and finish that lemonade." Her eyes focused on Mari with a sharp intensity.

Mari realized the old woman wasn't fooled a bit by John's explanation. Her heart beat with hope, despite her concern for the couple's safety.

"No, I'm afraid we can't. I really need to get my wife home. Put her to rest." His grip tightened on Mari's arm.

Agnes laughed. "She isn't a dog, Mr. Hoover. Just a few minutes, please. Let your wife finish her sandwich."

Carl must have picked up on his wife's silent message because he reached back and opened the screen door. "We'd be honored, Mr. Hoover. It might be easier to get your wife home safely if she's relaxed."

Tension radiated down John's arm into Mari's. She held her breath, praying for the opportunity presented to her. Through gritted teeth, John agreed and released his hold on her arm.

It was all she needed. She spun, withdrawing her hand from her pocket. The hand clutching the rock smashed into John's forehead. As he fell, she snatched her purse from his hand. Before he hit the ground, she clutched her weapon in her right fist.

"I'm so sorry." She tossed a glance toward Agnes and Carl. "I really am. But he isn't my husband. He's a killer. Don't be here when he gets up." Mari stepped over John and riffled through the stunned man's jacket pockets until she located his handgun. She withdrew it and stuffed it into her purse. "Please don't tell anyone I've been here." She bent to retrieve the keys to the SUV. "And there's a car down that path. Could you see that it's returned to its owner?"

The couple nodded, their hands entwined in unity. "You go, sweetie." Agnes waved her on. "We'll make sure you get a good head start before we let this man go."

"I hope I haven't put you in danger."

Agnes released her husband's hand and stepped to the edge of the porch. "Don't worry about us. Take the old logging road that runs behind the house. It'll get you to Interstate 40. Might take longer, but there won't be any traffic."

"I don't know how to thank you." Mari's throat hurt from the effort it took not to cry.

"No need. Now git."

Mari's last sight of Agnes was of the woman standing over a fallen John, her hands on plump hips. *Bless you, Agnes.* She turned and sprinted for the waiting SUV.

The key turned easily in the ignition, and the vehicle's rear tires flung gravel as it surged forward toward the logging road. Although her heart beat rapidly from fear, her partially full stomach and quenched thirst helped her relax as she drove. She stopped by the abandoned car to fetch her suitcase, then sped down the road.

She had no delusions that John wouldn't follow her. He worked for someone, but she couldn't remember who. Was it possible she'd never met the man responsible for the assassination ring? Yes, she remembered. They'd always received their assignments by phone. The money had been automatically deposited into their account.

For a second, she considered going back and forcing John to reveal the identity of his boss. The ring needed to be stopped. But after she'd seen her daughter; assured herself she was safe. She'd keep her distance. No one would even know she'd been there.

The tires ate up the distance to the Interstate despite the holes and ruts in the road. Mari's head ached, and every joint in her body felt sore from the bouncing. She'd expected more from the SUV. Only the best for John, he'd always told her. Wishbone suspension, tinted windows, and fine leather seats. The only thing the seats were good for was helping her perspire in the rapidly climbing temperature.

She shifted. Her shirt stuck to her back. The heat caused the blood on her clothes to smell rank. She cranked up the air conditioner and rolled down the window. The first order of business for the day would be to change into clean clothes.

Just before the turn onto the interstate, sat a small farmhouse complete with a red barn and chicken coop. Marilu smiled at the sight of freshly washed clothing flapping on a clothes line. She needed things other than what she'd hastily thrown into her suitcase.

Her gaze scanned the yard. No cars or trucks in sight. She cut the engine and slid from the seat, grabbing her purse from the passenger seat.

A young beagle ran barking from under the wooden porch, causing her to keep one hand on the door of the SUV. "Hey, little guy. Anyone home?"

The dog whined, wagging its tail and wiggling its way to her. "Fearsome beast, aren't you?"

She patted the dog's head, then strode to the clothes flapping the breeze. She sent a thanksgiving prayer heavenward as she noticed several items of women's clothing. Scooping the clothes into her arms, she again ran her gaze over the yard. What she wouldn't give for a shower. She gnawed the inside of her lip.

Taking a deep breath, she marched to the porch, up the stairs, and tried the door. Locked. She eyed the dog, then strode to the back of the house. No doggy door. She really didn't want to break a window. She'd be leaving cash for the clothes, but wasn't sure the cost of a broken window wouldn't cost more than what she was willing to spend.

She laughed, the sound ringing across the quiet yard. An honest assassin? Who would have thought?

To her delight, the back door swung open easily at her touch. *Trusting people. Ought to be more careful. You never know who might waltz in.*

The dog followed her inside and promptly made a beeline toward the garbage can. Mari headed out of the kitchen and into a small living room. A hallway branched to her left. Halfway down the hall, she discovered the bathroom.

Depositing the clothes on the toilet lid, she adjusted the water in the shower to a comfortable temperature and dropped her filthy clothes in a pile on the floor. The underwear she hung over the shower head. She felt almost giddy as she stepped beneath the shower's spray. She could be surprised at any moment by the home owners, but the opportunity to wash away the day's grit was worth it.

A shampoo sat on the lip of the tub and she lifted it to smell the scent. Strawberry. Mari lathered, then washed her

23

body with a bar of Dove. When she'd finished, and feeling a bit foolish, she scrubbed her underwear with the soap. Wet underwear would be better than none at all. Feeling like a new woman, she stepped from the shower and perused the clothes on the toilet.

A blue and white sprigged sundress, jeans, a checkered shirt, two tee shirts and a pair of tan capris. She pulled the jeans over damp underwear. They were a bit big, but nothing the belt she'd taken off the back of a chair couldn't take care of. She donned a red tee shirt and gathered the rest of the clothes back into her arms.

Having wasted too much time already, she darted back to the kitchen. A pad of paper and a tin can with an assortment of pens and pencils sat next to the phone. She laid the clothes across the kitchen table, pulled twenty dollars from her purse, and wrote a quick note extending her apologies and thanks.

A door to her right proved to be a pantry, and Mari tossed another twenty on the counter. She located an empty cardboard box from the back porch and filled it with soda and staples.

The unmistakable sound of an automobile driving on gravel reached her ears. Mari froze. The beagle lifted its snout from the over-turned trash can, bayed, and rushed toward the front window.

CHAPTER FIVE

With her arms wrapped around the box, the corners digging into her upper arms, and her purse hanging around her neck, Mari barged out the back door. The screen banged shut with a sharp clatter. She cringed. As she turned her head to glance over her shoulder, a man marched around the corner of the house.

Mari's heart seemed to stop as time slowed, then clicked backward. It couldn't be. Surely the ring had completed the job they'd finished with her and Jack. The pastor she'd failed to shoot stopped and stared at her, his arms loaded with firewood. How could it be possible that the very house she steals from should be the man she'd been paid to kill?

Dark hair curled around the top of a white tee shirt. Arms bulged beneath the load they carried. Faded jeans covered muscular thighs. He'd changed a little since he'd been in the sights of her gun. That man had been dressed in Dockers and a polo shirt. His hair combed back from his face. This man looked like he'd stepped from the pages of Rugged Magazine.

"Hey!" He dropped his load of wood and charged after

her. "Drop that box."

With her weapon not being accessible, Mari did the only thing left to do. She ran for the SUV. Her pursuer caught up with her before she could open the door and wrapped his arms around her waist, lifting her off her feet.

"Let me go! You don't understand. You're going to get us both killed. You've got to let me go." Kicking him was like knocking against a concrete wall. It didn't faze him.

He lowered her to her feet and clutched her arm tight enough to leave a bruise. "Not a chance, lady."

Dropping the box of food and clothes, Mari reached for her weapon. Her captor was faster. He yanked the strap of her purse, hooked a foot behind her knee, and before she could blink, Mari laid flat on her back staring in astonishment at the man leaning over her.

"You've got a Glock? *And* a 357 Magnum?"

She'd forgotten the name of the weapons, just not the feel of them in her hands, or how to use them.

The man peered into her purse. Retrieving the Glock, he trained it on her. "Get up. You've got some explaining to do."

"Please. You're wasting time. I left money for the food and clothes. I…"

Cold blue eyes glared at her. "I don't care. Get up."

"Fine." She glanced down the logging road, and, not seeing signs of pursuit, pushed to her feet.

This was not looking good. He should not take her into the house. Anyone found with her would be in danger. Mari was a fool. Sparing the time to take a shower, no matter how glorious it had felt, had been a mistake. Maybe he wouldn't know she'd almost killed him ten years ago. The hard glint in his eye led her to believe otherwise.

With the weapon poking her in the small of her back, he ordered Mari to pick up the dumped food and clothes and march ahead of him into the house. Taking a deep breath, she closed her eyes and bent. In the split second before rising, she barreled her shoulder into his waist, taking them both to the ground. The gun shot reverberated through the air.

Her element of surprise didn't last long. Before Mari knew it, she found herself lifted and banged onto her back, her captor straddling her ribcage. He held the gun inches in front of her face.

"Don't try that again."

What kind of pastor could fight like that or hold a gun in a woman's face? Regardless of the fact that she looked like a thief and attacked him first. He moved and Mari got painfully to her feet.

"Fine." She retrieved the discarded box and followed orders.

"Look, Mr. Morrison…" Once inside, Mari grabbed hold of the table to keep from falling. He shoved her into a kitchen chair.

"How do you know my name?"

"Uh, I…uh." *Oh boy.* How could she tell him she'd almost killed him?

"Well?" He tucked the pistol into the waistband of his jeans and leaned against the counter with his arms folded.

Mari's purse taunted her from the space behind him. "I'm waiting. How do you know who I am, and why are you robbing these people?"

"These people? You don't live here?" She narrowed her eyes. "Then what are *you* doing here?"

"I ask the questions. Who are you?"

How much should she tell him? Being a good person wasn't going to come easy. There were too many years before she knew what goodness was. She might as well tell the truth. Nobody would believe her anyway. "My name is Marilu Hutchins, and I'm on the run from somebody pretending to be my husband. Ten years ago, I was hired to kill you. I couldn't do it. A contract was put out for my husband and myself. He was killed. I woke up with amnesia, just remembering yesterday who I really am. My fake husband is now after me, and all I want to do is stay alive long enough to check on my daughter." There. It felt better to get it off her chest.

Apparently, the news couldn't have been more shocking had she told him Santa Claus was real or that she was the Tooth Fairy. He pulled up a chair and fell into it, his face pale. "Why did you want to kill me? I don't remember having ever done anything to you. I don't even know who you are."

"It wasn't personal. I was hired to do it."

"Not personal." He ran his hands through his hair. "When was this?"

"I told you. It was ten years ago."

He shook his head. "Couldn't have been me. I was … out of the country."

"You are Tom Morrison, right?"

"That was my twin brother. I'm Brad Morrison." He rose and paced the small kitchen. "Who would want to kill Tom?"

"I don't know." Starting to rise from the chair, Mari had second thoughts at the glare from Brad, and remained sitting. "I can't stay here. I'm being followed, and that puts you in danger. I only took the clothes because I was covered in blood and the food because…"

His head whipped around. "Covered in blood? Who'd you kill?"

"No one. I'm not a killer anymore. I broke…"

"Why not?"

"What?" This man could fire questions faster than any interrogator she'd ever met.

"Why aren't you a killer anymore?"

Releasing a deep breath, she answered. "I heard your brother practicing his sermon. I realized I couldn't kill a man of God. His message was about God's love and forgiveness. It hit me hard, and I accepted the message he was giving, even though he didn't know I was there. End of story. Except that by not killing him, I killed my husband."

"He knew." Brad shook his head. "Tom sent me a message to … where I was. It doesn't matter. He told me he thought someone was trying to kill him. Said he had information that couldn't get into the wrong hands. He'd spotted you through the slats of his office door."

"But he kept talking. Acted like everything was normal." *Information?* Things were turning strange, and having woken from what seemed like a ten year nap, Mari was having a hard time keeping up. "If he knew someone was after him, why didn't he go to the cops?"

"I don't know."

"He's a pastor. They're supposed to do the right thing." Of course, the right thing would have gotten her arrested, but she was trying to change her ways. After she saw Jeanna, she'd turn herself in.

"He wasn't perfect." Brad pushed away from the counter. "I've got to figure out what to do with you."

Wasn't perfect? "Where's your brother now?"

"Dead. Almost ten years ago." Brad rubbed a hand over the stubble on his chin. "He died when his church caught fire."

"An accident?"

The glare he cast her way would have skewered a boar.

"I wasn't there, but fires don't leave a bullet in someone's head. Look," he planted his palms on the table and leaned into her face, "I do *not* want to discuss this with you. The only thing I want to do at this point is to figure out what to do with you."

Relief flooded through her, leaving her limbs weak. She breathed slowly in through her nose and out her mouth. A fresh fragrance of rose came from the vase of yellow buds in the center of the table. "You aren't turning me over to the cops?" Leaning to the side to get away from him, she spotted her purse, left unguarded.

Brad's nearness made her uncomfortable. Blue eyes sparkled like star bursts beneath dark lashes and thick hair that ached for a woman to run her hands through it. Still mourning for Jack, she had no intentions of falling for a man, much less one she was beginning to dislike.

The beagle barked from where it had taken refuge behind the sofa. Recognizing an opportunity, Mari lunged for her purse as Brad turned to glance at the dog. By the time she clutched the weapon, Brad had the other one aimed back at her.

"Well, this is an interesting turn of events." One corner of his mouth turned up.

"How so?" As Mari circled around him, he mirrored her, dancing with her in a crazy slow dance of two people ready to kill each other.

"This is ridiculous," he said.

"Just put the gun down. I'm a professional." Well, not anymore, praise God, but she wasn't going to stand still while this man shot her, or worse, turned her over to the authorities. Her heart beat with such intensity, she was certain he could hear the pumping.

"I can handle a gun." Even in Mari's confused state, the man looked good. Like a warrior. His inky hair tousled around his head, tee shirt painted on with perspiration, and the beginnings of a five o'clock shadow on his jaw.

"Who are you?" Her gaze settled on the weapon in his hand. From the way he gripped the handle, it was easy to see that a gun felt familiar to him.

"That doesn't matter. Lower your weapon."

"You first." This was ridiculous. "On the count of three."

Brad laughed, the sound low and full of mischief. "You're an assassin. I can't trust you."

The window in the front room exploded, littering the floor with colorful prisms of glass. Pieces of rainbow rained down. Brad and Mari dove as one beneath the kitchen table.

Before the gunfire ended, the beagle had joined them.

"Stay down." Brad placed a hand on her head, pressing her closer to the floor.

"Don't touch me. I can take care of myself." She slapped his hand away.

Footsteps pounded on the front porch. Aiming her weapon toward the front window, Mari duck-walked around the kitchen counter.

"Where are you going?" Brad grabbed a fistful of her tee shirt, pulling her off balance.

"To see how many there are." She shrugged free. There was no more gunfire as she continued her duck imitation, but two men's voices drifted through the shattered window. One voice was John's. She stopped before crunching across the glass shards and alerting them to her immediate position.

Backtracking, she spotted Brad standing with his back flat against the wall, weapon held at the ready. He motioned his head toward the back porch and held up two fingers. With the two men out front, it was obvious John had obtained help.

What was hidden inside this head of hers that these men so desperately wanted?

"Now what?"

Brad shrugged at her quiet question. They'd have to come up with a plan quick, because the men would be inside soon, and Mari didn't want to shoot anyone. At least she and Brad were no longer holding their weapons on each other.

Her pulse pounded in her ears. Although the skills came back to her in a rush, the feelings and emotions were new. For ten years, she'd been Stacy Hoover. Less than twenty-four hours and she was back to being Marilu Hutchins, running for her life, and preparing for a shoot-out against the man she'd thought was her husband. Life definitely had a way of throwing curve balls, and since she was so new into the God thing, she felt clueless as to what the next step should be.

"If we go out shooting, we're dead. If we stay in here, we're dead." Brad stepped to her side.

"I'm not crazy about the odds."

It felt good for him to be by her side, even though she didn't know him and they'd come close to shooting each other mere moments before. Anything was better than going it alone. She felt a twinge of guilt at the thought of an innocent man being dragged into the situation. After all, he'd only been chopping wood until she showed up.

"I can distract them while you get away."

"Excuse me?"

As they talked, they backed away from the windows and doors until they stood shoulder-to-shoulder in the hallway.

"You didn't ask to be here. They're after me. It isn't right for you to be involved in this."

"I'm more involved than you know. I'm involved because of Tom. You're a surprise to me in all this. We'll get out together."

His answer raised questions. She was determined to get to the bottom of who Brad Morrison really was. But first, escape.

"Okay, here we go." Brad went back to the kitchen and whipped a quilt from the back of the sofa, knocking a vase of flowers to the floor. He ripped a hole in the fabric with a kitchen knife, then covered them from head to foot with the quilt and headed toward the door.

"Are you crazy? They'll kill us." Mari shook her head.

"They won't know which of us to shoot. I'm hoping one of us is valuable to them, and I'm thinking that person may be you."

"Wait. My purse and suitcase." She snatched them from the counter. "And the food." After she returned with her arms loaded, Brad readjusted the quilt.

With her heart in her throat, Mari allowed Brad to place an arm around her shoulder, holding her close as they stepped out the back door. The faint scent of his cologne caused her blood to race, and she realized it'd been a long time since she could remember being attracted to a man.

The knowledge saddened her. Had she felt anything for John during the years she spent as his wife? She hadn't been happy. She'd known something was missing in her marriage. Her heart told her she'd loved Jack, but the void of the last ten years dulled even that feeling.

Curses filled the air as they marched off the porch toward the SUV. Brad hunched his frame to Mari's height as they headed across the yard. She couldn't see out the hole, and had to put her trust completely in the stranger beside her. Imagining John's fury, she smiled.

CHAPTER SIX

Bullets kicked up the dirt around their feet and flew up the legs of Mari's jeans, stinging her ankles with pricks from tiny pebbles. The arms holding the box shook, and she realized how foolish it had been to worry about a box of food and clothes. She tried to draw upon the cold-bloodedness of her past, and failed. She leaned into Brad. He tightened his hold around her shoulders and quickened their pace.

"Marilu!" John's voice rang across the yard. "We *will* find you. You'd better have what I want."

But she didn't have a clue what he was talking about. Her head throbbed from the information flooding back into it, and the enormity of how much information she still lacked. Her body shook with the force of her heart's pounding, and she perspired beneath the faded quilt.

Although the trek across the yard took only minutes, it seemed like an hour of walking a gauntlet. The tires of the SUV, the only part Mari could see beneath their covering, never looked more welcoming.

Brad opened the driver's side door, shoved her inside, causing her to spill the box on the floorboard as she climbed over the gearshift, then climbed in behind her. "Stay down!"

He turned the key in the ignition, then threw the SUV into drive. They spun a donut in the yard of the country house, sending men with guns diving for cover behind parked cars and a well-house in need of a paint job.

"Yee haw!" Brad sprayed a round of bullets from the Glock and flung gravel as they sped down the drive and onto the highway.

After peering over the seat to see two sedans speeding after them, Mari sat firmly and hooked the seatbelt across her middle. "Really? Yee haw?" Somehow that didn't seem like something that would come out of his mouth. She glanced behind them. "They're coming."

"I figured they would." Brad whipped the steering wheel to the right, taking them down a poorly graded dirt road. "But I know these hills better than the average man. I've been hunting them for years."

"Oh, you're a Bambi killer."

He frowned and bounced them down a road consisting of two tire tracks through tall grass.

"At least I eat what *I* shoot, most of the time. Unlike others in the car."

Well, La Di Da. Handsome or not, Mari didn't like him. She'd find a way to ditch him at the first opportunity. Staying with her would only get him killed anyway—by either herself or those chasing them. Preferably not herself.

Confusion reigned supreme. Having accepted the Lord only three days before being shot, Mari had no idea how to proceed after waking with her memory returning. Training showed she had the required skill to end someone's life. Her reluctance to do so, and squeamishness at the thought of actually accomplishing the act of an assassin, told her something wasn't yet clear in her muddled mind. Except that she hated killing. That she knew without a doubt.

All she wanted to do was sleep. Or cry.

Brad glanced at her. "What's wrong with you?"

35

Was he dense? "Excuse me?"

"You look like you're going to cry."

"Crying is for the weak."

Mari's teeth clunked together, and the top of her head almost met the roof of the vehicle. She yelped and clutched the hand strap hanging on her right. The outside scenery passed in a jumpy green reel, like a misaligned movie tape, speeding past at a speed that couldn't be considered safe.

"Slow down or we're going to crash."

Brad swerved to avoid a collision with a huge oak tree. "If we slow down, they'll catch us. If we stay far enough ahead, we have a chance of losing them."

"You're enjoying this." The thought was hard to conceive, but the face splitting grin on the man's handsome face confirmed his enjoyment.

"As long as there aren't any flying bullets, why shouldn't we have fun? This vehicle is a sweet ride."

"Because those men will kill us the first chance they get!" Crossing her arms, Mari glared out the window and muttered, "I may have just woken up yesterday, but I'm not foolhardy enough to ask to be shot."

"Neither am I. Thus, the need for speed."

He spun the vehicle toward the left, down a trail filled with potholes, fallen saplings, and rocks the size of cantaloupes.

It wasn't clear to Mari why she felt safe in the presence of this stranger. He clearly knew how to use a gun. He also knew she'd been hired to kill his brother. What would prevent him from returning the favor? Despite the circumstances of them being thrust into each other's company, she relaxed. For the first time in twenty-four hours, the tension left her shoulders. The road smoothed out as they rejoined the highway, and she slept.

"Wake up, Sleeping Beauty."

The truck stopped in front of a cheap motel. The flamingo pink building made a horseshoe around the cracked parking lot. Paint peeled from the stucco like skin from a leper. Letters were missing from the sign, announcing the place as Horse hoe Moel.

"Wow. Nice place." After peering over her shoulder for pursuers, Mari shoved open the passenger door and slid from the SUV. Across the street lay a mega-store. "I'm going over there while you check us in."

Brad's gaze followed hers. "Not on your life, sweetheart. Where you go, I go."

"I'm not going to ditch you."

"Of course you aren't." He grabbed her elbow and steered her across the street. "What's so important? Didn't you steal everything you needed from Mrs. Parker's house?"

"Whose house? Besides, it isn't stealing if you leave money." His grip on her arm wouldn't loosen, no matter how hard she tugged. "I need some hair dye, toiletries, and bullets. A small hunting knife wouldn't hurt, either." It would fit perfectly in her boot. It should have pained her to see how little he trusted her, but she didn't trust him much either.

"Morbid shopping list."

His arm wrapped around her neck as she sidestepped and tried to turn into him with a roundhouse kick. "None of that Martial Arts stuff, Lu Lu. We're going into the store, getting what you want, and waltzing back out like a couple of sweethearts. Got it?" His arm tightened.

"Got it." Mari would obviously need to be trickier with her physical attacks. The man had training.

Brad loosened his hold and reclaimed a grip on her arm as they entered the store. Fluorescent lighting and a child's shrill screaming greeted them. Having enjoyed the status of being John Hoover's wife, Mari couldn't remember the last time she'd set foot in a discount department store. The noise seemed a bit overwhelming. She halted just inside the door.

"Keep moving." Brad propelled her forward with a push to the back. "It won't take long for your friends to find us."

They stopped first in the aisle of hair products, and she chose a shade of strawberry red. She prayed it wouldn't turn the expensive blonde streaks in her hair a ghastly shade of orange. Strange thought, considering she was running for her life. If she were dead, it wouldn't matter what color her hair was.

After grabbing some toothpaste, toothbrushes, a backpack, and deodorant, Brad and Mari headed to the sporting goods department. A short line formed at the counter. With her arms full, Mari got behind a heavyset man who smelled of diesel fuel and body odor.

"This isn't going to work." Brad glanced behind them. "The line is going to take too long."

"A distraction?"

"Give me some money."

"Why can't you use your own money?"

He held out a hand. "Because this whole mess is your doing. If I hadn't run into you, I'd be happily taking care of Mrs. Parker's home while she's in Florida. Blissfully unaware that such a person as Marilu Hutchins even existed. Besides, my wallet only holds twenty bucks. Now, when I step to the front of the line … do something. Anything to get the attention on you and off me."

"Then why the clothes on the line?"

"She hung them right before she left. I was going to take them in." He shook his head and turned away.

The only kind of distraction she knew to make consisted of guns blazing. Somehow, she didn't think that would work here. Gnawing the inside of her lower lip, Mari glanced around. A man in a cowboy hat stepped behind her, tipping the brim of his hat when she glanced his way. With a smile, she turned back to face the front, and swooned.

With the ease of a rescuing hero, the man caught her, lowered her to the floor, and shouted in a deep baritone for help. Soon everyone within close proximity bent over Mari, peering down with concern on their faces. From the corner of her eye, she could see Brad conversing with the sales clerk. Each time the man glanced her way, Brad steered him back to the subject at hand. Within minutes, he'd rejoined her, parting his way through the sea of concerned onlookers.

"Oh! Sweetheart!" He winked as he squatted next to her, pulling Mari close. "Are you all right?" Brad glanced up at the crowd. "My wife is expecting our first child. She gets dizzy every once in a while. Nothing to worry about." He pulled her to her feet.

Mari nodded. "He's right. I'm fine. Just, uh, pregnancy … stuff."

With one hand on the small of her back, Brad led her to the front of the store. The flesh beneath his hand burned, making her conscious of his touch. How long had it been since a man had touched her? What had her marriage with John been like? Amazing that she couldn't remember. It seemed like the moment Mari remembered who she was, she'd forgotten most of the last ten years of her life. Sorrow flooded through her again as she thought of Jack.

The memory of him seemed to fade more with each hour. Her heart ached at remembering that during their last moment together, he'd been angry with her for accepting Christ. If only she'd been able to open his eyes to the truth before he died.

Mari laid the products she'd gathered on the belt in front of the cash register. Brad stayed so close to her side, his body heat threatened to sear her. His breath on the back of her neck sent spiders skipping up her spine. She stepped back heavily, stomping on his foot. "Move back," she hissed.

He lowered his head, bringing his lips close to her ear. "So you can escape me? I don't think so."

She turned her head to stare into blue eyes dotted with flecks of gold. The movement brought his lips too close for comfort. She jerked back. His soft chuckle raised the hair on the back of her neck.

After they paid for the items, and Brad hung the plastic

bag containing them over his wrist, he ushered Mari back to the motel. She felt like a cow being shepherded by a dog. A big mean Doberman. Her temper burned close to the eruption mark.

Maybe if she shot him in the foot? One glance at his muscled physique ruled out that option. He'd probably still outrun her.

A bell tinkled over the door of the manager's office, and Brad held out a hand for more cash. To the man's credit, he hadn't planned on a day like today and, therefore, was short of cash. At this rate, she wondered how long hers would last.

Then it occurred to her that she would be sharing a room with a stranger. A very good-looking one. Her mind went off in a completely different direction. Her face flamed again, making it difficult for her to believe that she could ever have been a cold-blooded killer. Yet … she shook her head. The ache from too much information returned, and Mari wished she'd bought some aspirin.

After following Brad from the office, she hesitated in the doorway of a hideously orange room. A musty odor assaulted her, and she took a step back.

"It's not the Ritz, but it's home for tonight." Brad nudged her inside. "Not shy, are you?"

"No." Mari breathed a sigh of relief at the sight of two beds. "Why didn't we just go to your place? I don't think John has a clue to your identity."

"Well…" Brad pulled up a chair from a rickety table beside the window and straddled it. "Have a seat, Lu Lu. I've something to tell you. It seems I have a few secrets of my own."

CHAPTER SEVEN

Great. He's a lunatic in blue jeans. The mattress squeaked as Mari perched on its edge. Her gaze flicked to her purse.

Brad's laugh rumbled through the room. "Relax. You might want to shoot me when I've finished, but wait until I finish anyway." He took a deep breath. "I'm Brad Morrison. Identical twin to Tom Morrison…"

"Not identical, but almost," she muttered.

He chuckled again, throwing back his head. "I'm way more handsome, right?"

Her cheeks flamed.

"My cover business is owning a construction business. I actually work for the FBI, where I spent the last two years undercover in Mexico."

"FBI!" Mari bolted to her feet and dove for her purse. Brad was quicker.

"Whoa!" Wrapping his arms around her waist, he hauled her to her feet. "Let me finish. You may like what you hear."

Hammering the man with both feet didn't seem to faze him, so she tried a backward head butt. All that accomplished was to have him increase the bear hug he had on her and cut off her breath.

"Marilu, stop it or I'll knock you unconscious and tie you up."

The tone of his voice had the same effect as a gallon of ice water. Mari stiffened, and froze. "I can't go to prison until I've seen my daughter."

"Promise me you'll settle down, and I'll finish my story."

With no other apparent choice, she resumed her seat on the bed. "I promise."

"Marilu…"

"I promise. I said so, didn't I? If nothing else, I'm a woman of my word."

"Okay." Brad picked up the chair he'd knocked over in his haste to prevent her from retrieving her weapon, and straddled it again. "I spent the last two years undercover in a Mexican prison. You don't need the other details. Just know that I'm not in a playful mood after *that* experience. In between other aspects of my job, I've been trying to find my brother's killer. That, and the reason they killed him. Then you stumble into Mrs. Parker's yard and into my hands." He tapped his temple. "There's something stored up there, Marilu Hutchins, that will blow this case apart."

"But I don't remember much of anything."

He laughed again. Anger simmered in her. How dare he laugh?

"That's obvious." Brad folded his arms across the back of the chair and rested his chin on them. "You help me find out what it is these guys want, and I can get you a pardon."

Hope leaped in her chest. "Even for murder?"

"Well…" He winked. "You haven't actually committed murder. From what I've been able to gather, my brother was supposed to be your first hit, and as you know, you weren't able to go through with the job. You can't even be arrested for attempted murder."

"But my skills. The things I can do. I remember seeing dead people. People I thought I had killed."

"You were trained very well, Lu Lu. Thank God you never had to use them to actually kill anyone. You were most likely present while others did the killing."

Thank God, indeed. This delectable morsel of information choked her, sending Mari into a fit of sobbing so severe, the bed shook. There were no words to describe the emotions flooding through her. Nothing that could amount to the massive feeling of relief. The weight of the universe had just been lifted from her shoulders upon knowing she wasn't a murderer. She would deal with the fact she was an accomplice later.

Brad obviously didn't know how to respond to a woman armed with tears instead of a weapon. He hadn't moved since dropping his bomb of good cheer. His brow wrinkled, and even through her veil of tears, Mari could see the compassion and helplessness on his face.

"Lu Lu…"

She held up a hand to halt his words. "Sorry. You can't imagine the guilt I've lived with since waking up yesterday morning. And don't call me Lu Lu."

"Can't promise that, since I have a tendency to give people nicknames. I've given you a good one, compared to some others I've come up with." Brad moved from the chair to her side and laid an arm clumsily across her shoulders. Although she appreciated the gesture, his arm lay like a heavy beam. Then, his attempts at patting her in consolation were more like he was trying to stop her from choking.

"Thank you." She shrugged his arm off and grabbed the bag with the hair dye along with the top clean tee shirt from the box. This time in a shade of sky blue rather than red. "I'm heading to the bathroom to emerge a new woman."

As ammonia fumes filled the bathroom and her plastic glove-covered hands smoothed coloring solution through her hair, she pondered her predicament. First of all, she had to admit to being afraid. Very much so. There was so much she couldn't remember.

How could she not have known she wasn't a murderer? She'd had every intention of pulling the trigger on Tom Morrison. Some would say God's hand had stopped her. She prayed it was so, and that He hadn't forgotten her while she'd been sleeping.

When Mari stepped out of the bathroom, she joined Brad as a redhead. His eyes widened almost as much as his grin. "I like it. Very nice. Fiery temptress suits you."

"It's not that red." The comment made her flush with pleasure. She'd always been proud of her dark blonde hair. Jack had loved it. He'd said her fairness complimented his dark. Her positive with his negative.

Brad rummaged through the box she'd grabbed from the farmhouse and withdrew the makings of a sandwich. All she'd managed to grab was peanut butter and jelly. Not her favorite.

"The feast of kings." Without the benefit of utensils, Brad plunged his fingers into the peanut butter and slathered it onto the bread. He then did the same with the jelly.

Mari's stomach churned. "I'm not hungry."

"Come on, Lu … Marilu. I washed my hands. Things are going to get tough over the next few days. You've got to keep your strength up." He grinned over a giant bite of his sandwich.

"No, thank you." The bed beckoned, and she propped the two thin pillows against the hard headboard. Sleep wasn't going to come easy, but she had plans to try anyway.

"I see the wheels churning in your head." Brad plopped across the opposite bed. "Your plans cannot be anything that doesn't include me. Like from the book of Ruth: Where you go, I go."

"Is that in the Bible?" Uncomfortable against the headboard, Mari slid until she lay prone, the pillows bunched beneath her head.

"Yes." Brad followed suit with his own pillows. "I'd forgotten you're not familiar with the good book."

The lamp between the beds outlined him in profile, softening his jaw line and highlighting each mahogany curl with gold. He was a beautiful man. Where Jack had been chiseled from marble, Brad had been whittled from a piece of warm wood. Mari tried drudging up feelings of love for Jack, something other than guilt over his death, but they'd died along with the old her. Jack was dead, Brad was here with her in the tacky hotel room, and yet she still felt very much alone.

~

Brad watched her sleep. Maybe she wasn't a murderer, but she was an accomplice to such and a thief. The fact that she could hardly remember what happened before yesterday rankled and left him feeling like he was being tossed around in a dryer.

Every time he moved on the hard mattress, her eyes popped open and fixed a stare on him, severe enough to have sent Charles Manson running.

She might be the prettiest woman he'd seen in a good long while, and have some skills that would put most men to shame, but he still didn't trust her not to stick a knife in his back and take off with the car. It was going to be a long, sleepless night.

Flopping back on the bed, he folded his arms behind his head and stared through the dark room at the ceiling. He suspected the reason the men were so hungry to capture Marilu was because she held all their names in her head, whether she remembered or not. Someday, she might remember everything. It was Brad's job to make sure she lived long enough.

When the FBI hadn't found her body next to her husband's ten years ago, they'd thought maybe she'd crawled off and died in the woods. They'd combed the area for days. No one suspected she'd been living practically next door. What had her life been like during that time? Had John Hoover kept her a prisoner in her home? How else could she have gone undetected for so long?

Why had they kept her alive? They could have killed her and ensured she didn't tell anyone of their identities. Unless … they thought she already had. But who and when? Her parents, perhaps?

No, the assassination group would have thought of them. Marilu's family must have no part in her former career. If not them, then who had the information vital enough to keep Marilu alive?

The case involving her death had been closed a long time ago. Brad grabbed his cell phone off the nightstand and stepped outside the motel room. Prickles on the back of his neck alerted him to the fact that Marilu watched with her intense blue eyes.

Outside, he punched in the numbers. "It's Morrison. I've got Marilu Hutchins in custody."

"You're kidding. Where's she been hiding?"

"Right under our noses. She's had amnesia for the last ten years, and is married to one of the other assassins. Right now, she remembers very little." Brad paced the cracked sidewalk, keeping one eye on the motel door. It opened a couple of inches.

"Do you believe her?"

"I do. I'm taking her to the safe house for now. If her memory is returning, I want to keep her under close watch."

"So, I guess you're back from vacation." His partner chuckled.

"Looks that way. I'll keep you informed." Brad clicked the phone off and went back to the room.

Marilu had rolled over, her back to the door. So, she'd heard his half of the conversation. He shrugged. The two of them might as well be as upfront with each other as possible. They'd be spending a lot of time together.

CHAPTER EIGHT

Somehow, Mari slept. Restless and tangled in scratchy bed sheets. Dark dreams of being chased through a tunnel with no idea of who she was. It was with a sense of relief that she woke.

The morning sun squeezed through the water-spotted curtains, dotting the room with prickles of light. Her stomach growled, making her regret passing on the peanut butter and jelly sandwich the night before.

"I can hear that from over here." Brad's hair stuck out in all directions as he rolled from the bed. "Let's grab something from a drive-thru and get back on the road."

"Do you have any idea of where we're headed? My parents live in the mountains, right?"

Brad stiffened. "You can tell me where they live later. There's a safe house about an hour from here where I can get something clean to wear, and we can get more weapons."

Her heart stuttered. "I don't want more weapons."

"Believe me, we'll need them before we're through."

"What if I never remember what we're looking for?" Would she have to run for the rest of her life? Would she ever hold her daughter again?

"You will." Brad lifted the box of food. "Have faith, my dear. It's just not going to happen as soon as we'd like." He smiled. "I could knock you in the head, if you wish. A knock to the head to forget, another to remember."

"No thanks." She glared, remembering the conversation she'd eavesdropped on the night before. He might be acting like a concerned friend, but Brad was nothing more than her captor. It would do her good to remember that.

Brad opened the room door leading outside as if he expected someone to be waiting. His shoulders tensed beneath his tee shirt. Before following him outside, Mari withdrew her Magnum 47 from her purse and clutched it in her fist. Brad pulled his weapon from the waistband of his pants.

"I wish you'd leave that box behind." Brad opened the passenger door to the SUV. "Or at least leave it in the vehicle until you need something out of it. You need to keep your hands free in case we're fired on."

Why *did* she carry the box? Did it provide a security she felt was lacking? Something solid to hold on to? She would never take her past, should she remember it, for granted again.

Sliding into the vehicle, Mari leaned back and tossed the box on the back seat. "My dragging the box with us provided you with dinner last night. I didn't hear you complaining then."

He raised an eyebrow and tossed a crooked smile in her direction. "Testy this morning, aren't we?"

Not being a morning person, it didn't help that she'd skipped dinner the night before. Now, with a plunging blood sugar level and an escalating headache, Mari dared anyone to step out and shoot at them. Contrary to her desire not to kill anyone, this morning she might change her mind. Beginning with the handsome stranger with the infuriating grin next to her.

They pulled into a hamburger joint, and Brad took the

liberty of ordering ham and eggs between an English muffin. Two for Mari and three for him. Her hips grew fatter just at the thought of eating one at the same time her mouth salivated. It'd been years since she'd eaten anything close to fast food. Keeping trim had always been a priority. John had insisted she look and act a certain way.

The food tasted heavenly. Greasy, full of flavor, and it settled in her stomach like a boulder. Still, it filled her.

Once they hit the curvy mountain roads, nausea rose, rolling and boiling in Mari's stomach. Another thing she seemed to have forgotten, her tendency toward motion sickness. She hung her head out the window and panted like a dog.

"You okay?"

"I'm going to hurl." She reached for the door handle.

"Real lady like." Brad steered the SUV to the side of the road just in time for her to tumble from the vehicle and kneel in the dirt. He leaped from the SUV and rushed around to hold back her hair while she lost her breakfast. Wow. She hadn't realized he had a gentlemanly side to him.

Then, to make matters worse, Brad grabbed her once again around the waist and pulled her behind the protection of the SUV's door. His flinging her around like a mop doll was quickly becoming a habit she didn't care for. She wished for more strength than was in her five-foot-three frame.

John sped by, spraying bullets from a forest green sedan's window. Until that moment, she'd had no idea John's SUV had been bullet proofed. Another prayer of thanks flew heavenward.

"I love this truck." Brad slid to the ground, clasping her tightly to his chest. When there came a lull in the gunfire, he released her, dove into the front seat through the passenger door, pulling Mari in after him. "Get your weapon. Fire it out the window, and hold on."

The smell of rubber drifted through the open window as

they peeled away from the shoulder of the road. Brad maneuvered them into a crazy game of head-on chicken with John.

Massive SUV to sedan faced off in the center of the road, engines racing and tires squealing. Mari's trembling hands couldn't hook the seatbelt across her lap fast enough.

"Forget the seatbelt!" Brad placed a hand over hers. "You need to be hanging out the window and firing."

"Are you crazy?"

"No, they are. There's no way that truck can win in a head-on collision with this vehicle."

The SUV surged forward. Brad twisted the steering wheel, taking them in a swerving pattern, trying to dodge the bullets zinging off their fender. "Get out the window!"

"Yes, boss." Mari's fingers closed around the butt of the weapon. The feel of the handle brought back a flood of memories. Her hand steadied as she perched on the door, her legs balanced on the seat. Her torso twisted through the window. Pressing the trigger, she shattered the windshield of the other automobile then aimed for the tires.

"What are you doing? Shoot the driver."

"No. I won't take the chance I might kill someone." Just the thought almost made her lose her precarious seat on the windowsill.

"It's them or us, sweetheart."

John's face grew clearer as the vehicles raced toward each other. How close would they get before one swerved away? Who would lose their bravado first? Mari's guess was it wouldn't be Brad.

For one moment, her gaze locked with John's as she aimed her weapon for his heart. His crooked grin told her he knew she couldn't pull the trigger.

She shifted her aim and squeezed.

Minus a tire, the other vehicle careened off the road and into the thick trees. In one fluid motion, Mari rejoined Brad inside the cab. "I did it. Without killing anyone."

"What you did was allow them to continue hunting us. Mark my words, Lu Lu, they won't have the same hesitations about killing us." He placed one large hand on her knee and squeezed. "You did good, princess."

Pride rose more than just his words could invoke. For that one moment, she had wanted to kill John with an intensity that frightened her. But she'd overcome and still managed to help them escape. Yes, Brad was correct. They'd be back, but killing them was one less thing she'd have to face God about.

"Do you think John knows where this safe house of yours is?" She chose to ignore his comment about princess. The guy seemed to receive enjoyment from riling her. She wouldn't give him the satisfaction of knowing how his nicknames annoyed her.

"No, I don't think he has a clue. Very few people know about it, including most agents."

"Not everyone has access?" She fished in her trusty box for a bottle of water. One thing she hadn't managed to bring. The sour taste in her mouth had her dying for a drink of anything. She grabbed a soda.

"On a need to know basis. Safer that way."

Trees zipped past on each side of the highway. The wind swooshed through the open window. Mari drifted to sleep.

A hard jounce down a dirt road and her head knocked against the door, waking her. Having slept, she hadn't had any recurrence of motion sickness, but the banged head could give her stomach a run for its money.

Afternoon sunlight imitated dusk as it filtered through the heavy foliage forming a canopy over the trail Brad called a road. The woods were silent except for the crunch of limbs and the banging of rocks under the SUV. Through her open window, Mari caught a whiff of something fishy and mossy.

Secluded didn't begin to describe the location of Brad's safe house. They drove at least an hour down that rough path before he stopped in front of a small log cabin nestled beneath oak and pine trees. Smoke swirled from a chimney. A pond shimmered behind the cabin.

"Stay in the car." Brad rested his hand on his weapon.

"Maybe it's another agent." She copied Brad's actions without releasing her seatbelt.

"Maybe." He pushed open the driver side door and stepped cautiously from the vehicle. With another glance of warning for her to stay put, he proceeded to the front porch of the cabin. With his back against the wall, Brad peered through the front window. A grin split his face, and he waved her forward.

Then, with a yell, he kicked open the front door and barged in with weapon pointed. Whoever he surprised, responded with a yell, then a laugh. Using caution, Mari stuck her head around the corner.

Brad had another man wrapped in a bear hug and lifted off the wood floor. "Oh, man, how long has it been?"

"Too long. Put me down, you idiot. We spoke on the phone this morning." The man turned his head and spotted Mari. "Who's the doll?"

"This is Marilu Hutchins." Brad held out a hand toward her. "Come on in, Lu Lu. This is an old buddy of mine, Rick Baylord."

Rick's expression was confusingly bland as he walked toward her. Regardless of feeling as if he knew exactly who she was, she held out a hand for him to shake. The man clasped it between both of his and bent his curly blond head over them. For a moment, she expected to feel his lips caress the top of her hand.

"It's always a pleasure to meet a looker such as yourself."

Her eyes were in danger of getting stuck in the back of her head, she rolled them so far back. "Ditto." Rick was handsome with thick wavy hair and dark chocolate eyes, but Mari wasn't crazy about narcissistic men.

He kept his grasp on her hand and led her to a battered leather sofa, cracked and dry with stuffing poking from several holes. "And what brings such a lovely lady to this neck of the woods?"

"Lay off her, Rick," Brad growled. "We've got people after us, and Marilu isn't interested in your Casanova act." He straddled a rickety wooden chair. "What brings *you* here?"

"I'm looking for someone." Rick motioned his head toward Mari. "Can't tell you now. I only stopped here for a place to chill for a bit."

"How long's a bit?"

"One night, maybe two." His gaze flicked to Mari. "Could be persuaded to linger longer, though."

"I'm not interested." Realizing she still held her weapon clutched in her fist, Mari stuffed it in the waistband of her pants.

"Oooh." Rick winked at Brad. "She looks hot as fire, but she's as cold as ice. I like that in a woman."

"What is there to eat around here?" Brad stood and swung the chair back to the table.

"The cabinets are pretty well stocked. Someone's been here recently."

"I'll find something." Mari's stomach growled as she escaped to the corner assigned as the cabin's kitchen. One counter ran in an L-shape. A chipped goldenrod stove sat next to a clunking refrigerator of the same color. After rummaging for a couple of minutes, she discovered cans of stew and a large pot.

It didn't take long to have dinner bubbling happily over the burner. She kept her ears trained on the men's whispered conversation. They apparently had no idea how good her hearing was.

"So, who are you looking for?" Brad's deep voice rumbled softly across the room.

"The Ice Queen. Looks like I found her."

"Marilu? What, somebody didn't trust me to bring her in?"

If it had been possible, her ears would have perked up higher. She resisted the urge to turn around and instead, concentrated on stirring the stew with a long-handled wooden spoon.

"Hey, man. I'm just telling you what my orders are. I was heading into town to pick her up. Now, I don't have to."

"I'm not ready to take her in." A chair creaked. "She's got something hidden in her memory that can solve this case. I'm holding on to her until I find out what it is."

"No way. You'll be putting yourself in danger."

"Part of the job."

Rick groaned. "Man, I'll try to cover for you, but I don't know. It'll be hard. We'll both probably be in trouble. Nichols will have our badges. Maybe you should call him. Where you two headed?"

"To see her kid. I figure the more familiar places we visit, the better her chances are of remembering."

The spoon dropped into the stew, splattering hot sauce over her knuckles. Mari gasped and lifted her fingers to her lips. Why was Rick looking for her? Earlier, Brad had said he didn't know where her parents lived. Had he been lying?

Bowls were stacked on a shelf above the sink, and she reached up to grab three. Who was the bad guy here? Was Brad only using her to get to John, or did he really want to help?

"Stew is ready." Mari clunked the bowls a little too roughly on the table. "Sorry." Using a napkin, she wiped what she'd spilt.

Brad's gaze rarely left hers as they ate. He answered Rick's continuous chatter with monosyllable's. Mari squirmed beneath his attention and concentrated on supper. Despite coming from a can, the stew tasted delicious.

When she rose to clear the table, Brad took the bowls from her hands. "I'll help you."

Rick pushed back from the table. "Guess I'll go look around outside."

Once he'd gone, Brad turned back to her. "What's up, Lu Lu?"

"Nothing." She took the bowls from him and placed them in the sink.

"Uh-huh."

Turning, she leaned against the counter. "Why are you helping me exactly?"

"I don't understand."

"I feel like I'm just a way to solve this case. Like you're tagging along for the ride. I know Rick's been looking for me. I overheard you two talking. What I want to know is why?"

Brad shrugged.

"Really?"

"He said he'd been given orders to bring you in. That's all I know." He leveled those gorgeous blue eyes on her.

"I know enough that I could go out on my own. I could take care of myself."

"I know that." He curled his hand around her arm. "Sit down. Let's talk this out."

"I'd rather go to sleep."

"Fine." He dropped his hand. "You can have the sofa."

"Great." She stormed across the room and grabbed a dusty afghan from the back of the sofa. "What are you doing?"

Brad spread across the rug at her feet, his arms behind him cradling his head. "Going to sleep."

"Not there, you aren't."

"I am, unless you want company. Rick doesn't take no for an answer very well. He's a great agent, but rather loose in morals."

"I'll sleep with my gun."

"You do that." He didn't move from his spot on the floor.

A spring poked her in the leg when she flounced on to the sofa. If she'd been a cartoon character, steam would have poured from her ears.

Locusts and frogs serenaded outside the window. Brad moved occasionally, and Mari felt a momentary twinge of guilt at his feeling as if he needed to protect her. She was a trained assassin after all, even if a mistaken one. Even if she hadn't actually ever killed anyone, she had no doubt she knew how. Darkness had completely cloaked the room by the time she fell asleep.

CHAPTER NINE

Chubby cheeks and bright blue eyes danced in front of her. Mari's arms reached for her daughter, only to have her skip away. She smiled at the innocent picture she made.

The day was shattered by the sound of gunfire. Her baby girl fell, limp, to the grass.

Tears streamed down her face. She wailed and bolted from the sofa. Her hand gripped her weapon as she turned in the darkness, searching for the shooter. Something struck her below the knees. She fell.

"Marilu. It's me."

Brad straddled her, and she bucked beneath him. "Get off me!"

"Not until you settle down."

His face appeared pale. The moon cast shadows behind his head. "You're dreaming. There's no one here."

Her chest heaved with sobs. Tears soaked her hair. "They killed her. I saw her die."

Brad rolled off her, then pulled her beside him onto the sofa. "Who killed who?"

"They killed my baby. My Jeanna."

"It's just a nightmare, Lu Lu." His strong hands were tender as he smoothed her hair from her face.

"It seemed so real."

"It wasn't." He sat up, pulling her into his arms.

Regardless of how she felt about him, she snuggled close. When was the last time someone had comforted her? "How do you know? They killed Jack. They tried to kill me. They're still trying."

"You're safe as long as you have something they want."

Brad pushed to his feet, taking her with him. "Let's have some coffee."

She followed him to the table and pulled out a chair. He moved around the counter in his bare feet as silent as a ghost. Within minutes, he sat a mug of hot coffee in front of her.

The steam rose like a wraith in the dark kitchen. The events of her dream still left Mari shaken, and she wrapped her hands around the warm mug to steady them.

An image of God, obscured by her lack of knowledge of Him, rose in her mind. The need for a deeper relationship with the Creator drew forth a thirst for comfort so deep the coffee could not quench it.

"Do you have a bible?"

"Yes," Brad said. "Here and at home." After placing his mug across the table from her, he made his way to a small end table where he withdrew a small black book from its drawer.

"I suggest you start in Psalms. If it's comfort you're wanting, you'll be able to relate to King David."

Nodding, she stood, gathering her coffee and the Bible. "Thank you."

The sun was just beginning to peek over the mountain when she stepped onto the front porch. What better place to get acquainted with God than smack dab in the middle of His creation?

Alone with God, except for the birds, and despite

knowing Brad and Rick were separated from her by a log wall, instead of alarming Mari, the thought reassured her. She was perfectly safe, unless a sniper had her in his scope from the camouflage of the forest. But this was a safe house, and she chose to believe it to be so.

She scanned the trees, and seeing no cause for alarm, opened the Bible. If someone did have her in their sights, then go ahead and shoot. She was already tired of running.

The book fell open to Psalm 69. When her gaze landed on the words, *Save me, O God, for the waters have come up to my neck,* she knew she'd found exactly what she needed. Her eyes skimmed over the page, devouring every morsel she could draw from the words.

By the time Mari reached, *Come near and rescue me; redeem me because of my foes*, the tears poured forth in a torrent. God's presence washed over her, and although she didn't feel any wiser, she definitely felt more loved. She felt ready to conquer her foes and find her daughter.

Rick walked up a path to her left, clearly surprised to see her so early in the morning. She admitted to being curious herself, that he was out. Having expected him to be in bed after checking the perimeter the night before, his sudden arrival outside stirred up a pot of curiosity.

"Good morning, beautiful." His smile looked forced.

"Good morning."

"What are you reading?"

"The Bible. Read it?"

He put a hand over his heart. "Please don't tell me you're a bible thumper like Brad."

"I'm proud to say I am." Or at least she was trying to be.

"Why?"

"Why not? I like knowing there's somebody greater looking out for me."

"I'll look out for you." Rick plopped down on the porch next to her.

"No, thanks. I'd rather rely on a sure thing."

"Your loss, sweetheart." He stared toward the pond west of the house. "You don't need somebody you can't see. I'm here, and Brad's here."

Mari stood and clutched the Bible to her chest. "Look, let's stop the charade. I heard the two of you talking last night. I know why you're here. You'll have to shoot me in order to take me in. Why is my nickname the Ice Queen?"

"Word on the streets is you can shoot someone without blinking an eye."

"That isn't me. You've got the wrong woman."

"Seeing you standing there with a Bible makes me believe I just might be wrong. Or it could just be a clever act on your part." Rick stood and dusted the seat of his pants. "Only time will tell, I guess. If I don't wake up dead because you've murdered me in my sleep, then I'll be more inclined to believe you."

She bit her tongue, turned her back on him, and headed to the pond's edge. Why get into a verbal altercation with a man who already had his mind made up? Not that she blamed him. Since she knew so little of the woman she used to be, she had no ammunition to defend herself with.

The morning sun cast diamonds across the placid surface and Mari wished she could stay there forever with her daughter at her side. She strained to know what was locked in her memory. *Please, God. Reveal to me the secret that is hidden. It could save lives and put away forever those responsible for a ring of murder.* It wasn't lost on her that turning in the assassination ring would mean turning in herself. It was a sacrifice she was willing to make. But first, she needed to lay eyes on Jeanna to reassure herself that she was safe and that her parents were protected.

It dawned on her that she also had a bargaining chip with the FBI. Secrets revealed in exchange for her family's protection. Maybe even amnesty for one Marilu Hutchins.

~

"What do you mean she wasn't hired to kill my brother?" Brad rubbed his hand through his hair. Why had his boss kept such valuable information from him?

"I'm sorry," Bob Nichols, head of the FBI division Brad worked for, sighed. "The information was on a need to know basis."

"This was something I darn well needed to know." To find out that Marilu was actually hired to protect his brother, and failed, did nothing to raise his esteem of the woman. "You're telling me that she works for us? Then what in the world was she doing with Jack Hutchins?"

"Pretending to be married to the guy in order to infiltrate the ring. The pastor that married them wasn't ordained, so they were never married. Although, Jack didn't know that, and, the child is his. Marilu chose to keep her pregnancy even though it was conceived during her job."

Brad's world tilted, but no more so than Marilu's would when she remembered she wasn't a paid assassin. Instead, she was hired to keep the ring from killing Tom until the others could find out what someone had told him in confidence during a bible study. What would this news do to her already muddled brain?

"We don't want you to tell her any of this. Let the memories return on their own. As long as the ring thinks she is one of theirs, it may provide her some protection."

"They're trying to kill her!" Brad thrust to his feet and paced the path through the trees.

"They're trying to kill you. Make sure both of you stay alive. I'll send you her file. Check your email." Click.

Brad stared at his cell phone. What a mess everything had become. It might have been better for all of them if Marilu had stayed dead. He shook his head, remorse filling him. He couldn't wish death on anyone, but life had been simpler thinking that his brother's killer had also died. He glanced toward the cabin.

Marilu passed by the window. She'd undertaken the job

of cooking for the three of them without argument. Sounded fine to Brad. Rick could barely boil water, and if Brad had to concentrate on making sure toast didn't char while his brain raced through the news of the last few minutes, he'd burn out his last brain cell.

Needing a few more minutes of solitude in order to muddle through the notion that Marilu worked on the same side of law enforcement he did, he set off deeper into the woods to read the file that had come through on his phone.

The sun filtered through the heavy tree limbs, dappling the path with spots of light. Birds twittered from the branches, flitting away as Brad got closer. He continued on until he came to a cliff overlooking a deep stream thirty feet below. His boss had landed a bomb in his lap. Nichols might have told him not to say anything to Marilu, but considering the circumstances, and her fragile mind, Brad would make the decision to say anything or not on his own.

He kicked a rock. It sailed into the water with a plop. When the last ripple faded to the bank, he turned and headed back to the cabin. How long would they need to stay at the safe house? Until Marilu's memory returned, or should they leave and flush out the assassin ring?

If he asked her, Marilu would say to leave. She wanted to see her family, even if it was from a distance. Not a good idea. If they were followed, her family would be in jeopardy. That brought another question to Brad's mind.

Why had her family been left alone all this time? Wasn't it possible that Marilu had told her parents the information locked in her memory before Jack Hutchins died? The idea held merit, especially now that Brad knew Marilu wasn't the ruthless killer he had believed her to be. The information they needed wasn't about the names of the assassination ring, but a list of agents trying to bring down the ring.

He had no idea what to do, except sit tight until something came to him that lessened their chances of being killed. As he approached the house, Rick got behind the wheel of a Ford truck and turned around to drive down the mountain. Lucky guy. He had nothing keeping him there.

Never one for inactivity, Brad's nerves already twanged from the anxiousness of doing nothing. He barged through the front door. "Where did Rick go?"

Marilu turned away from the sink where a pile of dishes sat on a towel to drip dry. "He went to town for supplies. Why?"

"Just wondering." Brad plopped onto the faded sofa and thumbed through some hunting magazines on the coffee table. "Remember anything yet?"

"No." She scowled. "It won't come because I want it to, Brad. It will come in its own good time."

"That could be too late."

She tossed the rag she was holding into the sink of sudsy water. "Well, excuse me for getting shot at and hitting my head on a rock. I'll try better next time." She stormed into the bedroom and slammed the door. The cabin shook from the bang.

Brad leaned his head against the back of the sofa. He was being a jerk. Of course she couldn't remember at the snap of a finger. He needed to find something to do to pass the time. He turned one of the magazines over and jotted notes with an ink pen he grabbed from under the stack of magazines. Marilu, FBI agent assigned to protect Tom. Infiltrated ring as a wife to Jack. He tapped the pen against his teeth. Tom had information given to him by a church member.

Ha! Some church member. Marilu possibly had the same information. Amnesia for ten years. What sparked the beginning of her memory returning? He tossed the pen down and headed to the kitchen for coffee. Marilu had left a fresh pot of hot water on the stove. He reached for a mug and a jar of instant coffee.

Drink made, he headed for the back deck and stared into

the trees. Storm clouds rolled across the sky, dark and pregnant with rain. The breeze kicked up, sending dry leaves skittering across the yard. Thunder rumbled in the distance. Brad would need to hunt up candles when he went back inside. Storms on the mountain often left the cabin without electricity.

He took a sip of his coffee as a squirrel scampered across the yard. Usually, Brad enjoyed the few days a year he spent there, but now, he felt none of the peace he usually enjoyed. Too many secrets. Too much unknown. He sighed and tossed the contents of his cup into a nearby bush.

Tomorrow, he'd do some repairs around the place. Anything to pass the time.

"What is this?" Marilu slammed through the door, high spots of color on her cheeks, and waved the magazine he'd written on in his face.

CHAPTER TEN

S hots rang out from the front of the house. Mari dashed back inside. Brad's footsteps pounded after her. Stuffing the magazine in the waistband of her jeans, Mari grabbed her gun. She plastered her back against the wall, praying the thick logs that made up the cabin would protect her, held her Glock at the ready, and craned her neck to peer out the window.

Rick raced toward the house, his truck flinging gravel. He drove as close to the front porch as possible, then scrambled from the vehicle. The moment his hand touched the front doorknob, a bullet caught him high in the shoulder and spun him around. Another took him in the gut. He fell inside the cabin.

"Get out!" He glared up at her. "What are you waiting for?"

Brad grabbed Mari's arm. "Let's go. We can't help him." He pulled a duffel bag, which contained weapons, from behind the sofa and shoved Mari ahead of him.

"We can't leave him." Tears blurred her vision. "He's your partner."

Sorrow filled Brad's eyes. "I'll deal with that emotion

later. You're my priority now."

"I'll hold them off the best I can." Rick scooted until he sat against the wall. Blood covered the front of his blue button-up shirt. "But it won't be long until they're after you. Go!"

"No, wait." She tried to dodge around Brad. "We have to take him with us."

"Stop!" He shook her. "We have to protect you. Don't make his death mean nothing."

She stared into his blue eyes. He was right. Rick had taken a great risk to warn them. Staying alive was all she had to give him in return. She brushed her hand across her eyes and returned the shaky smile he gave her. Rick blew her a kiss. Whirling, she dashed out the back door and into the thick forest behind the cabin.

The fallen pine needles and decaying leaves muffled their footsteps. The thick branches overhead cast the path she ran on into broken shadow. Brad thundered past her and off the trail, motioning for her to follow. She darted after him through thick brush and stopped at a quick-flowing creek. She leaped, her feet sinking into the thick mud on the other side. Brad pulled her out of the muck, and they continued their fast trek through the forest.

A stitch burned in Mari's side, but still she ran. All those days spent at an expensive gym wouldn't go to waste. She stumbled, but righted herself and kept running, focusing on her next breath, the next placement of her foot. Brad slipped back behind her, putting himself between her and their pursuers.

Why was she so important? She didn't know anything. She had woken next to a stranger, believing herself in love with Jack. Each minute that passed made her realize that too was nothing but a foggy memory. The notes jotted on the magazine stuffed in her belt told her that her remembered feelings for Jack were nothing but a lie. She choked back a sob and scrambled over a fallen tree. No, she'd felt something for him, despite his life of crime. She'd had his child.

"There." Brad pointed up a steep incline. "I'll cover our tracks."

She nodded and pulled herself up the cliff face, using bushes and imbedded rocks to help her ascent. Any moment she expected a bullet in her back. But no, they wanted her alive. It was Brad who faced the most danger. She glanced over her shoulder. He climbed with the skill of an outdoorsman, dragging a pine branch behind him.

She shook her head. That trick only worked in the movies. Still, it might buy them some precious time.

At the top of the cliff, she came face-to-face with the dark entrance to a cave. She started to enter and froze. Perspiration broke out on her upper lip and forehead. Her limbs trembled. She couldn't go inside. Not one inch. She bent over and balanced her hands on her knees to take deep breaths. In out in out.

"What's wrong?" Brad appeared at her elbow and propped the pine branch against the cave opening.

"I can't go in there."

"Are you claustrophobic?"

She nodded, her breath coming in gasps. "Who … knew?"

"Bend over more. Put your head between your legs." He guided her head down. "I'm sorry, Marilu, but we have to go in. It's the safest place around here to hide. I'll lead you just inside the entrance. You can see me the whole time I camouflage the entrance."

She jerked up. "You're going to close us in?" Her vision narrowed to a pin light. She swayed.

Brad caught her before she fell, and lowered her to the ground just inside the cave. "I'll be right back." He dug in his pack for a water bottle and handed it to her. "Focus on this."

Impossible. The more branches he moved in front of the

entrance, the less light she had to see by. How could she watch the weak rays of light filter through the bottle? She scooted until her back touched the cave wall. What if there was a bear inside? Or a cougar? What if John came and cornered them in there until they died of hunger or thirst, or their oxygen ran out?

Stop it, Mari! You'll be perfectly fine. Brad would come back any second and tell her everything would be okay. What was taking him so long?

"There." Brad crawled inside. "That should hide us."

"Are we safe?"

"For a while." He sat next to her. "How are you holding up?"

"I hate closed-in spaces. It's dark in here."

He twined his fingers with hers. "I'm here. I won't leave you."

Strange how a man she'd looked on as the enemy had become her strongest ally. The last few days were a whirlwind of emotions and information. She hadn't loved Jack. She wasn't married to John, legally anyway. Most likely not Jack either. Had she really pretended to be their wife as part of her job? What kind of woman slept with men as part of her job description? How could God ever look at her with love in His eyes?

Nausea choked her. She was evil, through and through. Maybe she shouldn't bother searching for her daughter. Jeanna didn't deserve a mother such as herself. Tears scalded her cheeks.

"Hey." Brad slipped an arm around her shoulders and pulled her head to his chest. "It will be all right."

"No. The things I've done … they're despicable."

"But you aren't that woman anymore. You're a new creation, remember?" He smoothed her hair as one would comfort a small child.

He was right. What mattered now was the woman Mari was at that moment. The woman she would be in the future.

A weight slipped from her shoulders. She pulled the magazine from her belt and placed it in Brad's lap. "I have some questions about your notes."

"You want to talk about this now? Before I start a fire?"

Mari straightened and scooted back. "Yes. We don't need a fire right this second. There is information on that magazine cover that I need to know. Some of it came back to me when I read what you'd written, but a lot still hasn't."

The cave lit with a bluish light. Thunder cracked. The clouds opened and rain poured outside the cave.

~

Brad had to raise his voice above the pounding of the rain. "I just found out myself, actually. You were hired to protect my brother. For so many years, I thought you'd killed him. I wanted nothing more than to meet you so I could repay you with a bullet."

It was hard to see the shivering woman next to him as a cold-blooded killer. Now, he knew she had the same intense combat training he did.

"As for Jack, well, you weren't really married to him, I guess."

"I can't believe the things I did as part of the job." She covered her face with her hands. "Why did the assassination ring hook me up with John?"

"My guess is that Tom gave you some information. You've stashed it somewhere, and they want it back."

She sighed. "I supposedly know who the agents are on our side. In the wrong hands, those agents are as good as dead."

"See?" He grinned. "You've remembered something." He had no doubt she'd remember where she hid the information. He needed to keep her alive until then. A task he prayed he was up to.

"I guess I did." She glanced toward the entrance. "It's getting cold."

He moved to the back of the cave. Knowing the

mountain like the back of his hand because of all the times he'd stayed at the safe house, he often came here to think over his latest assignment. For those times, he kept a stack of wood against the far wall. After gathering as much as he could carry, he set them near the cave's entrance. They wouldn't need to worry about smoke with the rain.

Soon, he had a fire started and the small cave started to heat. "You'll be warm in no time."

"Where do we go when we leave here? Is there another safe house somewhere?" Marilu scooted closer to the flames.

"In the city." He preferred the cabin, but since it had been compromised, he'd have to forgo the open spaces for the concrete jungle.

Now that they were safe, for the time being, he thought of Rick. He'd hated leaving him dying on the cabin floor. They'd had each other's backs more times than he could count. Rick had been a flirt and fun-loving, but a partner who could be counted on. He'd be missed by more than just Brad.

Brad fished his cell phone from his pocket. No service. Once they were off the mountain, he'd have to call Nichols and let him know about Rick's death and that he and Marilu were headed to safe house number two. He leaned his head against the rock wall of the cave.

How had Hoover known where the safe house was? Brad doubted Rick led them there. He had to have met up with them on the road leading to the cabin. Was it possible there was a mole in the agency? Nichols picked everyone personally, but it could still be possible someone had been paid to pass on information. Everyone had a price.

Even Brad. He'd almost cast aside his morals to have revenge on the woman who he believed had killed his brother. What if he'd acted on it upon first learning of Marilu's identity? He glanced to where she'd curled up next to the fire and fallen asleep.

Some cold-blooded killer she was. Afraid of small

spaces. Sick at the thought of what she'd been paid to do. A mistaken assassin. Nothing more. Yet, somewhere in that beautiful head of hers lurked valuable information and the knowledge of how to kill. He didn't want to admire her, but he did.

What if she reverted to what she'd thought she was: a member of the assassination ring? She'd been an undercover agent, after all. Anything was possible. Her memory could return full force and send her to the other side. Could he kill her then? He didn't know, but doubted he could. The two sides of Marilu Hutchins, the trained law enforcement officer and the wounded victim were at war in his heart. Which would emerge the victor?

He picked up a twig and poked at the fire's embers. He should sleep while he had the opportunity. No one would be searching the mountain for them in the heavy rain. He stretched out on the opposite side of the fire from Marilu.

"I'm sorry." Her soft apology drifted to him like a soft breath.

"For what?"

"Dragging you into the turmoil of my life."

"It's my job. Don't worry about it."

"You were taking care of someone's house. Who would have guessed that would be the one place I'd show up?"

Not him. It was almost as if their meeting had been engineered, planned by someone greater than them. Maybe it had. "We'll get through this."

"I want to see my daughter, even if it is from a distance." She shifted. The fire sparked, illuminating her face.

Brad met her gaze across the flames. So beautiful, so vulnerable. A strong need to protect her rose in his chest. He was a doomed man. Marilu wasn't the first woman he'd been assigned to protect, but she was the first to affect him so. "I'll try to manage it."

"Who is the father of my daughter? Not Jack, surely."

He shrugged. "You had her before … all this. Considering agents in our particular branch aren't allowed to have a family, I'm sure you signed over custody to your parents."

"Good. She won't be tainted by my past life." Marilu rolled over, putting her back to him.

Brad transferred his gaze back to the orange and blue flames of the fire. The smoke was sucked out of the cave and through the branches covering the entrance. The rain still poured, but had lessened in its intensity. He flopped to his back and stared at the ceiling. Roots penetrated the dirt. A scurrying at the back of the cave alerted him that something else had come in out of the rain. A rat, probably. Good thing Marilu was asleep.

They'd need to be up before the sun to sneak away before Hoover found them. Brad set the alarm on his watch, then placed another log on the fire. He willed his mind to relax, his breathing to slow. Once asleep, he could be awake in an instant if the need arose. He mentally pictured each part of his body going to sleep until his eyes closed to the sound of Marilu's gentle snores.

Good. She seemed to sleep soundly. Tomorrow would be another day on the run.

CHAPTER ELEVEN

When Mari woke, Brad was hunched over the fire with some type of skinned animal hanging off a stick. The smell of roasting meat alerted her to how hungry she was.

Brad glanced over and grinned, a dimple winking in his right cheek and sending her heart into a somersault. Seriously? The man was definitely an eyeful of man candy, but now was not the time for her to be thinking about how good he looked in the morning light.

She stretched sore muscles. "What time is it?"

"Five."

"In the morning?" She stared at him. "Where did you get that?"

"Caught it this morning. It's rabbit."

"I didn't hear a gunshot."

"Nope." His dimple winked again. "I did it the old fashioned way … with a stick."

You Tarzan, me Jane. Mari glanced toward the cave entrance. "The rain stopped."

"Yep. We'll have to get moving soon, before Hoover and his buddies find us." He cut off a chunk of the meat with a knife and handed it to her. "You have ten minutes."

Mari nodded and took her first bite of rabbit. Definitely didn't taste like chicken. Maybe ham with a bit of gamey wildness. Not bad. She wolfed it down and eyed the other half of the rabbit.

"We need to save this," Brad said. "We'll be in the woods for another day at least. Unless we get lucky enough to find an abandoned vehicle that runs, which isn't likely, or hitch a ride with some unsuspecting fool." He wrapped the rabbit in a piece of cloth before stuffing it and his knife into his pack. "Don't worry. I won't let you go hungry."

"I've been hungry before." She wasn't sure how she knew that, but somehow she did. She'd gone a day or two without eating before.

When Brad stood and slung his pack over his shoulder, she did the same and followed him outside. He stopped and crouched, surveying the surrounding area. All seemed clear and they started the slippery trip back to the forest floor. With all the sliding she did, Mari almost believed she'd lost her rigorous physical training as well as her memory. The seat of her pants and knees was coated with mud.

At the bottom, Brad held out a hand to steady her. Her hand felt small in his large, calloused one. He gave hers a squeeze, bringing a flush to her cheeks. For heaven's sake. She was acting like a silly school girl.

Brad set off at a brisk pace in the opposite direction of the cabin. When the path was smooth, they ran, when it was rough, they walked as fast as safety would allow. Occasionally, he led them through creeks for a ways, then back into the thick brush. Even with the autumn chill in the air, perspiration ran between Mari's shoulder blades. Despite the vigorous travel, she kept up, her breathing evenly paced.

Although John had kept a close watch on her during their "marriage", the one thing he had insisted on was regular trips to the gym. Why? Had he hoped she would never regain her memory and/or possibly join the assassination ring as she'd pretended? Otherwise, it didn't make sense for him to keep her at her physical peak. Not when she could beat him at hand-to-hand combat as she'd done the morning she woke to a new world.

She focused on Brad's strong back. His muscles rippled under the thin tee shirt he wore every time he moved a low-hanging tree branch. Why did she trust this man? He only wanted what was locked in her mind. She was nothing more than a job to him. Yet, she'd never felt safer in her life. Without a doubt, he would take a bullet for her.

Brad's cell phone buzzed, and he fished it from his pocket. "Seriously? It will be more dangerous with three more people. Fine." He shoved the phone back in his pocket and glanced over his shoulder. "Change of plans. We have to pick up some others before heading to the safe house."

"I take it that's bad news?"

"Depends on how you look at it. We're picking up your family. Their safety has been compromised."

Mari's steps faltered, and she tripped over a rock. Righting herself, she met his serious look. "What do you mean by compromised?"

He sighed. "They've been living in the witness protection program for the last ten years. Someone sent them pictures of them going about their daily lives. We'll be at their place in five hours, give or take a few minutes."

He turned, leaving her with her heart in her throat. She'd be reunited with her family during the most turbulent time in her life, that she could remember anyway. They must hate her for bringing all this trouble on them. She'd make it up to them somehow, even if she died doing so. With every fiber of her being, she'd use whatever training she'd received to protect them.

Despite the burning of her thigh muscles, she increased her pace and bypassed Brad. "Come on, slowpoke. Time is wasting."

He laughed and caught up with her. "You can't run for

five hours."

"I can try." The rumble of an engine drifted through the trees. She held up a hand. "Listen."

"Have you ever stolen a car before?"

"Yes. Just the other day, as a matter of fact, but I left the title to my Lexus in exchange."

Brad rubbed his chin. "A thief with a conscience. What do you have to leave this time?"

"I've a few stacks of hundred dollar bills in my pack." She grinned. "Courtesy of John."

He clapped her on the shoulder. "Then what are you waiting for? Let's find that road."

~

Brad hunkered down behind some thick brush, keeping Marilu behind him. A black SUV idled by the side of the road, John Hoover at the wheel and another man in the passenger seat. They seemed to be in a heated argument. A green sedan passed and honked, most likely upset that the SUV hogged the right hand side instead of parking on the shoulder.

"What are they doing?" Marilu whispered.

Her breath tickled his ear and sent his blood racing. She sent shivers up his spine every time she cast that blue-eyed gaze his way. There was no time for romance, especially with a woman he was assigned to protect. He shifted over a few inches.

"Arguing, I think." He straightened and moved closer to the road. The two men were sitting ducks. Now was his chance to take out Hoover before the man caused him and Marilu more anguish.

The vehicle roared away, flinging rocks and gravel into Brad's face. He put up an arm to shield himself. A rock pricked his forehead above his left eye. He put a hand to the spot and drew it away bloody.

"Here." Marilu dug in his pack for his knife, then cut off a couple of inches from the bottom of her shirt. "It's not the cleanes, but it will stop the bleeding." She tied the red strip around his forehead.

Wonderful. He looked like some caricature of Rambo. "Let's go." He stepped into the middle of the road. "We'll walk until a car comes along, then highjack it." He'd give the driver Nichols' number and have them reimbursed. Marilu's cash might be needed for something else.

As they walked, his mind drifted to Marilu's family. What in heaven's name was Brad supposed to do with a middle-aged couple and a young girl? He needed help, but with his partner dead, he didn't know of anyone else he wanted to work with. He cast a sideways look at Marilu. She would probably do as good of a job protecting her family as anyone. Maybe better.

An older model Toyota Sentra pulled alongside them. A young man, around twenty years of age, rolled down the passenger window. "Y'all need a lift?"

"Sure." Brad hated involving someone else, but if they could make the drive to the city quickly, they wouldn't have to steal. Hoover wouldn't be looking for them in a beat up car.

Marilu scrambled into the back seat while Brad climbed into the front. "We're heading to Placerville."

"That's where I'm going. I'm headed to work at Wal-Mart. I'm late."

"That's a good place to drop us off." Then they'd take a vehicle out to the farm. Brad relaxed against the back of the seat.

"Your car break down?" The young man reeked of marijuana. No wonder he was late to work. "You kind of look as if you were in an accident."

"Yeah, we ran into the ditch a couple of miles back," Brad said.

"Bummer. Hey, I'm Randy. Hold on." He pressed the gas pedal and the car stuttered before speeding down the road. "This old baby ain't much to look at, but she gets me where I'm going."

Brad forced a smile to his face. A black SUV headed their way from the opposite direction, and he slouched down in the seat. Hoover might not be looking for a car with three passengers, but there was no sense inviting trouble. He'd hate to get their pot-smoking friend killed.

Randy kept up a non-stop monologue on how he was working himself through school to be a pharmacist. Brad shook his head. A pharmacist with a taste for recreational drugs. A perfect mix. He turned and glanced at Marilu. Her eyes were closed, and her lips moved in a silent prayer. Good. They needed all the help they could get.

Having failed to keep his brother safe, Brad had no intentions of failing Marilu or her family. His job was one of the most important things he could do as far as keeping innocent people safe. He was good at it and planned on remaining at the top of his field. No killer such as Hoover and his group would get the better of him. Not while he had breath left in his body.

Thirty minutes later, Randy pulled into a parking spot as far from the store's front door as possible. "They don't like us to take up valuable space meant for customers." He grinned.

Marilu clapped him on the shoulder. "You're a good kid." She handed him a hundred dollar bill. "Lay off the pot, and make something of yourself." She opened her door and slid out.

Brad laughed and joined her, then shook Randy's hand. "Nice to meet you. Thanks for the ride."

"Wow. Cool." Randy pocketed the money and jogged toward the store entrance.

Brad scanned the parking lot for a nondescript automobile that would serve their purpose. Nothing that would attract attention, but something big enough for the crowd he'd soon be responsible for. "Start looking for a minivan with the keys still inside."

"People don't do that anymore." She scowled. "We'll have to find one where the husband is waiting for the wife to finish shopping. There." She pulled her gun and marched up to the window of a white van. "We're taking your car."

The pale-faced, overweight man joined them in the parking lot. "My daughter's in the back."

Brad flashed his badge then handed the man a business card. "Call this number. Ask for Bob Nichols. Tell him what happened, and he'll pay you back for the van. Get your daughter."

They waited, the man's gaze flicking from one side of the lot to the other before the man held a sleeping infant in his arms. Brad unhooked the car seat and set it beside the father. "I'm sorry. But we need this more than you right now."

The man nodded. "I hope you're on the up and up about paying me back."

"I am." Brad slid behind the wheel. He hated leaving the father and child standing in front of Wal-Mart, but time was of the essence. This particular father would live to see another day, Marilu's might not.

Brad glanced at her. "Ready to meet your daughter?"

She gave him a shaky smile. "No, but it's ten years overdue, don't you think?"

"I do." He backed the van from the space, tossed the father a wave, and headed back on the road. They had two hours to get where they were going. He prayed they would beat Hoover there.

CHAPTER TWELVE

Mari stared at her reflection in the hotel bathroom mirror. She'd see her daughter again in less than an hour. She tried to smooth the wrinkles from the expensive clothes she'd shoved into her bag upon leaving the house she'd shared with John. Somehow they seemed better than a stolen sundress. Pricey or not, the slacks and sweater looked cheap with the wrinkles, making her feel like a homeless person. She grimaced. She was homeless. She ran her fingers through her hair and wished for a brush.

A knock sounded on the door. "We need to go."

She opened the door and stepped out. "I look like a homeless person."

"You look fine." Brad handed her the Glock. "Hopefully, we won't need this today."

She shoved it in the waistband under her sweater, the cold metal as familiar to her as the worry in the blue eyes she'd studied in the bathroom. Grabbing her pack, she followed Brad out the door. Her steps faltered at the sight of a black SUV parked in front of their room.

"Don't worry," he said. "This one is ours. My boss had

it delivered this morning. I didn't think you wanted to show up at your parents' place in a stolen vehicle."

"Thank you." Tears pricked her eyes at his thoughtfulness, although she knew it was more than that. If they were spotted in a stolen car, the police would pull them over, endangering their lives as well as Mari's and Brad's. The man they'd taken the van from might not have trusted them enough not to report the vehicle stolen.

She stowed her pack in the back of the SUV then climbed into the front passenger seat. Her heart beat an unsteady rhythm, and she wiped her sweaty palms down the thighs of her slacks. What if Jeanna hated her? How mad were her parents at her for forcing them into a life of hiding? Now, this. They'd be on the run from a madman who wanted what was locked inside Mari's head.

She clicked her seatbelt into place and nodded to Brad that she was ready. He pulled onto the highway and headed north into the mountains.

"Witness Protection thought your family would be safer in a big city where they could merge with all the other people," Brad said. "But your dad insisted on a farm. Said he'd prefer to live as much off the grid as possible. He's done well. Hunts and grows his own food, traps animals, and sells quilts your mother makes. He even dug a well. Don't worry. They'll be able to take care of themselves."

His words were meant to reassure her, instead, her nerves jumped like live wires. Her father was a tough man, that she remembered, but was he also a man given to mercy and forgiveness?

Trees in autumn splendor flashed by in a rainbow of gold, pumpkin, and scarlet. In a ditch, the bloated carcass of a deer lay with stiff legs pointing toward the sky. Overhead, a hawk soared in search of a meal. How long had it taken her family to adjust to their new life?

qAn image of her father wrapping her in his arms returned to her. He'd been proud of her acceptance into the police academy. She'd never told him of her promotion to the secret agency within the FBI. Had he believed the stories of her turned traitor? She imagined him greeting her at his home with a shotgun.

"We're here."

Mari's breath hitched. On the porch of a single-story log-style cabin rocked a young girl. She looked so much like Mari, there was no mistaking it was Jeanna. "I'm scared."

"It'll be fine." Brad laid his hand over hers and squeezed. "I'm right beside you."

When they exited the SUV, Jeanna stood and went in the house to be replaced by Mari's stocky father. At sixty, he still retained his stiff military posture. In his arms, he cradled a shotgun.

She took a few steps closer, her heart in her throat. "Dad?"

"Is that my Mari?" He propped the gun against the porch. "Mary Ellen! Our girl has come home!" He rushed toward her and enveloped her in his strong arms. "My baby girl is home."

Tears coursed down Mari's face as she laid her cheek against his flannel-covered chest. The door banged, signaling her mother coming outside, and Mari raised her head. Except for the strands of gray mixed with the dark blond, her mother hadn't changed a bit. Mari rushed into her open arms.

"Oh, my dear." Her mom smelled of cinnamon and yeast. "Come inside and meet your daughter. We have a lot to catch up on."

Mari met Brad's gaze. He nodded and said something in a low voice to her dad. Mari followed her mother inside and came face-to-face with a younger version of herself. She stood, arms limp at her side, and waited for Jeanna to make the first move.

Jeanna took a deep breath. "It's like looking in a mirror, except for your red hair."

"That came out of a bottle."

"A disguise, then. Grandma and Grandpa told me you worked for the FBI and had to go into hiding like us. Are you here to stay?" She stood stiffly, her eyes shimmering.

"For a while." Mari opened her arms. "If you'll have me."

Jeanna moved woodenly into her hug. She accepted Mari's affection for a moment, then pulled back. "Do you want to see my room?"

"I would love to."

Mari followed her into a room large enough for a twin bed and a dresser. A colorful quilt was folded at the foot of the bed and nature scenes adorned the walls. On the dresser was a simple wooden jewelry box with Jeanna's name burned into the lid.

"It's lovely."

"I wanted rock star posters, but Grandma said no." Jeanna plopped on the bed. "Are you taking me away with you?"

Mari sat next to her. "Do you want me to?"

Jeanna plucked at a loose thread on the quilt. "I don't know you, so it might be kind of awkward. Can Grandma and Grandpa come?"

"I think we're all leaving." Her questions ripped at Mari's heart. What had she given up for the sake of her job? Could she get back everything she'd lost? "Why don't you pack a bag of the things that matter the most to you, and I'll be back in a minute."

~

"Your position here has been compromised." Brad wrapped his hands around the mug of hot coffee in front of him.

"What do you mean?" Dan Colson leaned his arms on the table. "We have to leave? I know someone is watching us, taking pictures, but—"

"Yes. I've been assigned to take the three of you, and Mari, to a safe house."

Dan met the startled gaze of his wife. She nodded. "I'll pack our bags." She hurried from the room, passing Mari, who entered the kitchen.

"There seems to be something locked in my head that certain people want." She headed to the coffee pot and poured herself a cup. "No one who knows me is safe."

Dan straightened, his face set in hard lines. He appeared as if he wanted to say something, but thought better of it. "I hate to leave my home, but I love my girls more than a herd of cattle and an old cabin. How far do we have to go?"

"A couple of days drive. I can't tell you more than that." Brad didn't know himself. He was still waiting for Nichols to inform him of a safe house that was vacant. He sipped his drink, then set it methodically on the table. "I can't say it's going to be easy. We've been shot at and hunted. I doubt that's going to change."

"I've faced danger before." Dan pierced him with the same blue eyes that were in his daughter's face. "Can you keep my family safe?"

"I'll do my best, or die trying." Brad met his stare.

"That's all I can ask." Dan pushed up from the table. "I've guns and ammo. I'll get them while the women pack food and clothes. We'll be ready in fifteen minutes."

Brad nodded and moved to the big glass window that looked over the front yard. He doubted Hoover knew where the Colson's lived, but he wouldn't put anything past the man. He seemed to be one step behind them, and Brad had a niggling feeling the department had a mole feeding Hoover the information. He needed to pay a visit to the office.

The pressure of looking out for an older couple, a child, and a woman with no memory weighed on him. What if he couldn't keep his promise to Dan? He meant he'd die trying, but what if that weren't enough? The assassin ring would kill everyone around Mari in an attempt to get her to hand over the information they wanted. Then, when they'd exhausted all means, they'd kill her, just as they'd done his brother,

Tom.

Mari stepped beside him. "We'll be fine. My family is strong."

"I know."

"Did Dad say whether I'd left anything with them?"

"No, and I didn't ask." Brad faced her, noting the sadness outlining her features. "If they have it, they'll say so. Now isn't the time to ask." He opened the door and stepped onto the porch. Outside, he pulled out his phone and called Nichols. "I have them."

"Head to Clarks. The safe house is on the outskirts of the city. Not a good area of town, but no one should think to look for them there."

"Sir, I'd like to come into the office before heading there."

"Why?"

"There's something I need to discuss with you that can't be said on the phone." Brad paced the porch, his rubber-soled gym shoes thudding against the wood. A brisk breeze blew down the collar of his shirt, and he shivered. "I wouldn't request a meeting if it weren't important."

"Very well. I'll see you tomorrow." Click.

"We'll all go with you." Mari stood in the doorway, her arms crossed.

"It would be better to leave you at a hotel."

"We don't get separated. Ever."

He grinned at the returning steel in her spine. Maybe they would all get through this nightmare. Dan pushed past them, a bulging duffel bag in his hand. He marched to the SUV and dropped the bag in the back.

"Mary Ellen, hurry up. Jeanna!" He stormed back inside, returning seconds later with five heavy coats. He shrugged at Brad's questioning gaze. "I believe in being prepared. We could get stranded somewhere."

"We're finished." Mary Ellen dragged a cart piled with boxes and blankets. Jeanna had on a backpack and pulled a rolling suitcase.

Brad sighed. He didn't fault them wanting to bring as many personal belongings as possible, but he preferred to travel light. "Don't worry about the farm. I'll get someone to care for it until you can return."

"You really think we'll be able to come back?"

"I hope so. Once we put the bad guys away, you should be able to come out of hiding." Brad helped them load their things, took one last look around the place, then got behind the steering wheel. So far so good. He prayed they could make it all the way to the safe house without an incident.

Dan climbed in the front, leaving the back seat to the women. In his lap, he rested the same shotgun he'd greeted them with. "What? Didn't you say we were in danger? I prefer to meet danger with a bullet and a lot of prayer."

"Me, too, sir. Me, too." Brad started the ignition and headed down the dirt road toward the highway.

The road was clear with no traffic in either direction. It would be sweet if they made it to a hotel without gunfire pinging the sides of the SUV. This had to be the most difficult case he'd ever undertaken. But, his name was on that list in Mari's head. The same list she'd hidden somewhere. He didn't relish being more of a target for the bad guys than he already was. He'd do what it took to keep them all safe.

On the highway, he increased his speed. In the rearview mirror, a vehicle matching the one he drove loomed closer.

"Down in the back seat."

CHAPTER THIRTEEN

Mari released a shuddering breath as the SUV behind them passed. A young boy waved from his car seat. False alarm. She shouldn't be so skittish. There was no way John could know where her family lived. Not unless someone told him or he'd followed without Brad, or her, noticing. Not very realistic, considering they were both on hyper alert.

She stared at the back of Brad's head. No. He wouldn't. He didn't seem to blame her for his brother's death. But what if he did? What if he harbored a secret vengeance and wanted revenge? Every one dear to her was inside that vehicle. He could take them all out at once.

If Brad was playing the part of a double agent, he now had everyone within his reach who could possibly have the list of agents. She closed her eyes, then snapped them open. She could no longer rest peacefully. If Brad reacted violently, her family wasn't trained to react in kind. She was. She pulled her gun and set it in her lap.

Mom turned in her seat. "Expecting trouble?" she whispered.

"Trouble is all around us." She glared at Brad through

the rearview mirror. His eyes widened when he met her gaze. Good. Let him know she suspected him. How else did John always know where to find them? He couldn't be that lucky, and following the faint trail they left would take him days.

They stopped a few hours later at a truck stop. Mari followed her mother and daughter through the gift store and into the restroom. They all three squeezed into the single room. Mari faced the door and kept guard. Now that she had her family, she wouldn't let them out of her sight.

Business complete, they went through the store and into a small diner where they met up with Brad and Mari's father already seated at a round table. Mari avoided Brad's questioning look and grabbed a plastic covered menu. She decided on biscuits and gravy.

When Brad left to attend to his personal needs, Mary Ellen elbowed Mari. "What is wrong with you?"

Mari sighed. "I don't know. All of a sudden I'm doubting Brad. The men after us seem to be steps behind us. As if someone is feeding them our information. What if it's Brad?"

"Don't be ridiculous." Mom frowned. "He's kept you alive this long, hasn't he? His agency has known our whereabouts for years. Your foggy memory is addling your brain."

"Maybe so." Her head pounded. Why hadn't he been straight forward about knowing where her family was? Clearly she wasn't thinking straight. Of course Brad wasn't a double agent. If so, he would have turned her in immediately. But what if he were waiting for her to remember where she'd hid the list? That niggling thought wouldn't go away no matter how she tried.

"You're still thinking about it." Mom straightened as the waitress brought their food. "If you don't trust Brad, then trust your father."

"You don't trust me?" Brad sat heavily in his chair. "Why not? You don't think I can keep you safe?"

Heat rushed to Mari's face. "It isn't that." She focused on the cooling breakfast in front of her. The stares of her family seemed to burn holes in her skin.

"Then what is it?" Brad crossed his arms. A shadow passed over his eyes.

She'd wounded him. Deeply, it appeared. Maybe she was wrong and confused. She rubbed her temples, willing the headache to go away. Who was she to judge whether someone was trustworthy or not? She could barely remember her past.

"You can request another bodyguard." Brad picked up his fork and stabbed the stack of pancakes in front of him. "I'm stopping by the office before heading to the safe house. You'll all need new identifications. You can put in a request then."

"No. I'm sorry. My head hurts so much I can't think, and thoughts whirl and tangle until I think I'll lose my mind." She shoved her food away. What was wrong with her? She'd had headaches early on in her "marriage" to John, but nothing in the last year or so. Could it be from the knock her head took all those years ago brought on by the stress of surviving? Nausea rolled in her stomach.

Brad's gaze had changed from hurt to concerned. He jumped from his seat and headed to the gift shop, returning a few minutes later with a bottle of aspirin. "This is all they had."

"Thank you." She popped two of the white pills into her mouth and downed them with a gulp from her water glass. She really was an idiot to think such a caring man wanted to hurt her. *Lord, bring back my full memory so we can put this all behind us.*

Jeanna had watched the interaction silently, her gaze switching from Brad to Mari as she ate her waffles topped with strawberries and whipped cream. What kind of example was Mari setting for her? First she'd accused Brad, now she sat in pain, clearly weak. Who was unable to protect their loved ones? Her. The thought that she could was ludicrous. She was the danger of the group, not Brad.

She forced herself to eat a few bites of breakfast. Every movement of her jaw was agony. She needed a dark room and quiet. Somewhere away from the clanking of silverware and calls from the waitress to the short-order cook. She fished money from her bag and tossed it on the table.

Where was John? Every time they stopped somewhere to spend the night, he'd shown up minutes later. Now, here they sat, in the open, in a public diner, and there was no sign of the man.

"I don't want to go to the safe house."

"Why not?" Brad's fork of food stopped halfway to his mouth.

"Every time we go somewhere, you make a phone call, and John shows up. No one needs to know where we go. Not even your boss. Give me your phone." She wiggled her fingers.

He dug it from his pocket and handed it to her. Mari stood and marched to the nearest trash can. She dropped the phone inside. They could buy a prepaid phone.

~ .

Although the thought of Mari not trusting him rankled, ate at his insides like a parasite, Brad admired her quick thinking. If there was a mole in the agency, it was not a difficult thing to trace someone via GPS. Although, he would have liked to give Nichols the heads up on a new phone number for calling him.

"I'll get us a phone right now, and then we're leaving." They'd stayed long enough in one place. The gift shop sold cheap phones. After purchasing one, he ushered the others outside into the SUV. They'd be at the office in an hour.

While he understood Marilu's reluctance to trust anyone, it hurt that she thought so little of him. After failing to keep Tom alive and well, Brad would do anything for this group with him. Why didn't she see that? Did she think he blamed her for his brother's death?

He had at first, but the assassination ring was bigger than anyone in the agency had previously thought. Only God could have kept Tom safe. Brad knew that now, especially since the stubborn-headed man refused to go into the witness protection program. Still, he should have been able to do something.

He glanced in the rearview mirror. Marilu had her eyes closed, her forehead wrinkled in pain. Still, she was beautiful. No makeup marred her smooth complexion. The red hair added to her paleness. While pretty, the color was nothing like the rich honey tone to her hair when he'd first met her. Maybe, under different circumstances ... No. He couldn't dwell on what-ifs.

The brown brick building with no sign, only the numbers 457 on the front, loomed over a cracked parking lot. Two cars occupied spaces. Brad pulled around to the back and entered the underground garage. If a person didn't know, they'd have no idea the building housed some of the smartest IT people in the country, or some of the world's most dangerous agents.

"Stay close and don't wander off," Brad said as he led his entourage into the building.

If someone walked in where they weren't welcome, they'd be locked into a room and interrogated for hours.

He settled the group in the lunch lounge before heading down the hall to Nichols's office. The muscled black man stood in front of his office window, hands clasped behind his back.

"Bob?"

Nichols turned. "So, what could you not tell me on the phone?"

"Speaking of phones, I no longer have mine." He scribbled his new number on a slip of paper. "Here's my new number."

Nichols frowned. "You think we have a mole." It

wasn't a question. In their line of work, only one thing would make an agent toss their department-issued phone.

"I do." Brad glanced through a second window that overlooked the IT lab. He spotted a new face. "Who's the kid?"

"Been here a couple of weeks. We recruited him right out of college. The kid is a genius with computers." He fixed his dark stare on Brad. "You know we scan everyone thoroughly. Why do you think someone is playing both teams?"

"John Hoover is always one step behind us. No more. Everywhere we go, he shows up within minutes. That isn't luck. Someone is helping him. I won't be heading to the safe house, either. I'm going to Ryan's cabin." Even with only the first name of his college buddy, Nichols would know where Brad meant. The name shouldn't mean anything to anyone else.

"How's Hutchins's memory?"

"Coming back in spurts. I think one of her family may have the information we seek, but I'm not asking until we're somewhere safe."

Nichols resumed his watch over IT. "I hate to think one of my men is dishonest. Was also sad to hear about Rick. He was a good agent."

Brad swallowed past the lump in his throat. "A good partner for sure."

"Do you want another one? Someone to help you babysit? Miller's back."

"Now, that's just cruel." No way in Hades did Brad want to work with his ex-fling, Sarah. Despite their professionalism, the tension would be thick enough to walk on. He didn't need that kind of distraction.

Nichols laughed, the sound booming through the plush room. "She said the same thing about you. Too bad, she's waiting. Probably already meeting your new friends. Even you need someone watching your back."

"I have Marilu."

"She's not in full capacity. When she is, she's one of our best, but for now, you're stuck with Miller. She's the only one I can spare right now."

Brad groaned. "I'll check in once we reach our destination."

He whirled and marched back to the lounge. Sure enough, Sarah was perched on a table, her shapely legs crossed, one swinging to and fro. Had she met Marilu before? A sliver of recognition shone in Marilu's eyes.

"Brad!" Sarah rushed toward him, planting a hard kiss on his lips. "I bet you never thought we'd work together again."

"I was hoping." He glanced at the others. "Ready?"

Marilu frowned, her gaze flicking from him to Sarah. She scratched above her eye, her attention focused on Sarah. Something triggered the beginnings of a memory. Brad needed to get her to safety before she collected it.

Despite the nasty disintegration of their relationship, Brad hoped Sarah wasn't the traitor. He'd hate to shoot her.

Back in the garage, he stared at the SUV. There weren't enough seats. His assignment got better and better. He sighed and signed for the keys to a dark green Suburban. At least it had been modified to have four wheel drive.

Sarah climbed into the front, leaving the others to scramble for seats. "I'm excited about this assignment. After the last one I had, babysitting will be a piece of cake."

Marilu snorted from behind her. "We've done nothing but dodge bullets and race through a thick forest. A real barrel of laughs."

"Really?" Sarah shrugged. "Okay, I was wrong, but I was really looking forward to something a bit easier."

"Wait. I remember." Marilu leaned forward, her face between the two front bucket seats. "I know where I've seen you before. You were dating Tom, Brad's brother, when he died."

CHAPTER FOURTEEN

Mari grabbed onto the seat when Brad swerved the vehicle into the ditch. Before any of them could collect themselves, he had his weapon pointed at Sarah's heart.

"Wait." Her eyes widened. She threw up her hands. "What are you doing?"

"Tell me you're the mole, and I swear you won't take another breath." Brad's cold words sent shivers up Mari's spine.

"I swear I loved Tom." Her eyes glistened with tears. "If Marilu knows me, if she remembers protecting your brother, she'll know that."

Did she? Marilu strained to remember, increasing the pounding in her head, despite the aspirin. As the one assigned to watch Tom, albeit from afar, could she swear that Sarah's intentions toward the man had been out of love?

"Well?" Brad twisted in his seat. "Mari?"

After she got over the fact that he'd used her nickname, Mari shrugged. "I think so. I can't remember. I just know she was there. A lot."

"Of course I was, you mindless moron. I loved him."

Sarah plopped back against her seat. "If I thought another knock on the head would bring back your memory so Brad wouldn't want to kill me, I'd hit you now."

"Watch your mouth." Dad's roar filled the car. "Law enforcement or not, you don't talk about my girl like that. Either you shape up or get the hell out of this car."

Mari opened her mouth, then snapped it closed. Dad never cussed. Ever. Things were escalating out of control and it was her fault. "Things are fine. Everyone settle down. Brad, I'm pretty sure Sarah wasn't there to kill your brother. I was watching, remember? I'd like to think I would've put a stop to her if she intended him harm." Instead, the bullet that ended Tom's life had come from a sniper Mari couldn't see.

Still, something teased the corners of her memory. Something that didn't ring true about Tom's death. Had Mari intended to go to those higher up to tell them … something? Tom's death had seemed too contrived. He'd been practicing his sermon, but acting as if he were waiting for someone. Then, Sarah had entered the room and lured him into a chair. Almost as if she'd purposely put him into position for the sniper's bullet. A hot and heavy make-out session. Sarah's lilting laugh as she'd asked Tom to wait in the leather chair. The chair by the window. The place he'd sat when the bullet found him.

Mari had been embarrassed from her watch point in an adjoining office where Tom practiced his sermons. Her ears had burned from the earpiece she listened through. When her gut told her something was wrong, she'd rushed toward the living room. Too late.

She eyed the back of Sarah's raven head as if she could find truth in the strands. She met Brad's gaze through the rearview mirror as he pulled the vehicle back on the road. She pressed her lips together and nodded. From the steely coldness in his return gaze, she could tell he understood.

"I need to use the restroom," she said. "This headache is making me sick to my stomach."

"There's a gas station up ahead. We'll stop there." Brad pulled onto the access road.

"I need to go, too," Jeanna said, as he stopped on the side of the building.

"You wait until I get back." Mari put a hand on her arm and squeezed. "Then Grandma can go with you."

"Sarah, go with her. Make sure she's safe." Brad turned off the engine.

"Sure, you trust me now." Sarah shoved open her door.

"You first." Mari waved the woman forward, hoping her combat skills wouldn't fail her now. The moment the bathroom door closed behind them, she reached over and flipped the lock.

Sarah's brows rose. "Seriously? Do you really think anyone is following us in here? Look at this place." She waved an arm around the dirty bathroom, pointing out the cracked mirror and stained linoleum. "This isn't exactly a prime meeting spot."

Mari pulled her gun from her waistband. "I remember a little now. About how you played Tom. Situated him in just the right spot to be shot. You're a good actress, playing the part of the grieving girlfriend. Too bad I remembered."

"You really have lost your mind." Sarah backed up, a smile tugging at the corners of her mouth. "No one is going to believe you over me."

"They won't have to." Mari advanced. "You won't be around to dispute anything."

"They should have killed you when they had the chance." Sarah lunged forward, tackling Mari to the floor.

Her breath left her in a whoosh. Her gun flew from her hands and clattered to the floor. She scrambled to her feet and wrapped her hands around the other woman's throat.

"Let me show you how crazy I really am."

"I'll kill you, same as that stupid preacher." Sarah kicked.

Mari jumped to the side, then slammed the other

woman into the tiled wall. Once, twice, she rammed her head into the wall, until Sarah sagged.

The woman reached under her shirt and brought out a Smith and Wesson handgun. "Your memories should have stayed where they were." She leveled the gun between Mari's eyes.

"What? And miss all this fun?" She dove for her gun. Her fingers wrapped around the handle. She rolled, squeezing the trigger.

Her first shot took Sarah in the thigh. Sarah's bullet went wild and embedded in the wall. She spun as Mari squeezed off another shot. This one took Sarah between the eyes, dropping her.

On her hands and knees, Mari fought to even out her breathing. Before she could get to her feet, the bathroom door was kicked open. Brad stood in the doorway, his gun in his hand.

"Are you okay?" He reached out a hand and helped Mari to her feet.

"Better than your old girlfriend. She admitted to setting Tom up." Mari leaned against the wall. "I don't think she's your mole, though. She wouldn't have had access to our whereabouts."

"I agree." Brad squatted next to her body. "But, she played a part in it all." He sighed. "I'll let Nichols know what happened."

Mari followed him back to the Suburban, avoiding the gazes of her family. She was nothing but a killer, regardless of which side of the law she worked on. The biscuits and gravy she'd eaten for breakfast soured in her stomach.

~

Brad hadn't wanted to let Mari be alone with Sarah, but he hadn't wanted the child, Jeanna, to witness possible violence more. It could have been Mari lying on that bathroom floor. She had guts, he had to admit. Failed memory or not, she hadn't forgotten her skills, and for that he was grateful.

He wanted to feel remorse for the death of someone who had once meant something to him. Instead, a grim satisfaction that one of the people responsible for his brother's death was now dead flooded through him. He filled their ride with gasoline while Dan purchased drinks and snacks, then Brad got them back on the road. There would be time to dwell on what had happened later.

"Where's the other lady?" Jeanna asked. "Why is my, uh, mom, in the front seat?"

"She isn't coming with us." Mari's voice was low, sad even. "She got … reassigned."

"That doesn't make any sense." Jeanna pouted until Mari's mother whispered something in her ear. The girl's eyes widened, then she nodded and stared out the window.

Brad turned his attention to the road ahead. Nichols had seemed reluctant to admit there might be a mole in the agency, but it made sense. Sarah could have known. It was unfortunate Mari had to shoot her. He cut a sideways glance. Mari still stared out the window. Tears trickled down her face.

She hadn't lost her skills along with her memory, but she'd regained remorse at killing. It was time for her to put in her official resignation with the agency. If not, Nichols would expect her to return to work once the file of names was found. While she'd be good at the job, her heart wouldn't be in it, and that could get her and her charge killed.

This job they had required killing on occasion, but they saved a lot more lives than they took. Lives of good people. The few bad ones they took out seemed worth the price to help establish justice in an evil world.

"You did what you had to," he said.

He started to pat her shoulder and pulled back. Physical contact was never a good idea with the person he was in charge of protecting. Feelings and emotions were not a part of the job.

"It's doesn't matter." Mari still didn't look his way. "It was me or her. Old habits die hard. I knew what would happen the moment I remembered who she was."

"Still—"

"Still what?" She turned on him with the ferocity of a badger. "It's okay that I killed someone? Not the first person I've put a bullet into, is it? That's who I am."

"Sweetheart." Dan gripped Mari's shoulder. "Your job is as a protector. You've done more good than bad in the line of work. Don't beat yourself up."

"This job has taken more from me than it's worth." She stared back out the window.

Sure, the job was tough, but every person Brad was able to save made it worth much more than the few things that went wrong. Evil stalked the world, and he and people like Mari were the warriors in the battle against it. If they stopped to dwell on every person who died at their hands, they'd be worthless as agents. He'd learned a long time ago that some things were out of his control. He handed them over to God and moved on.

"We're being followed." Dan turned in his seat. "Mary Ellen, get down." Mari's mother, sitting alone in the far back seat, slouched. "You, too, Jeanna." He propped his rifle on the headrest.

"Are you sure?" Mari peered through her side mirror.

"Not a hundred percent, but it's kept pace with us for quite a while."

Brad studied the vehicle through his mirror. Not the usual dark SUV. The road they were on had few turnoffs. The chance that Hoover had located them already was slim. Especially since he'd gotten rid of his phone. It had to be because of the Suburban. He'd checked it out at the office. It probably had a GPS tracker.

"We've got to ditch this truck at the first opportunity." How could he be so stupid? He'd jeopardized everyone in the vehicle.

"Another false alarm." Dan sat back down. "It's just a bunch of kids out for a ride."

The car passed them, teenage boys hanging out the windows and hooting.

Still, they needed to find a place to stop so Brad could disable the GPS, or find something else to drive. There. He swerved down a dirt road and parked behind some thick brush. "I need to check for a GPS."

Mari nodded and opened her door. "I'll keep watch."

Brad motioned his head for Dan to go with her. He popped the Suburban's hood and stared at the engine. What did a GPS tracker look like?

"Here." Dan handed him a black box. "It's a GPS blocker. Set that on your dashboard."

"Why do you have one of these?"

"Living off the grid. Sometimes, it's easier to have this than it is to disable the tracker on a vehicle. Then, if I want to resell, I haven't destroyed anything." He grinned.

"You're a man of mystery, and one I'm glad to have on my side."

Brad stuck the box through the window. At least now he didn't have to show his mechanical ignorance. "Everyone ready to get back on the road?"

Mari nodded and jogged back. Seconds later, a truck pulled onto the dirt road behind her. She ducked behind the Suburban with her family. Brad opened the driver side door and stood behind it.

Most agency vehicles, especially the ones used in protection of a witness, were bullet proofed, and if the man and the woman in the Dodge truck were unfriendly, he'd need protection. The doors of the Dodge opened and a large man in cowboy boots and jeans stepped out. He clutched a shotgun in his large hand.

CHAPTER FIFTEEN

"Y'all are trespassing." The man stopped by the hood of his truck. A big pie-eating grin stretched his mouth, but the cold look in his eyes set Mari back.

Mari moved to the door and set her Glock on the seat, shaking her head at Brad, who had taken a step toward the man and woman. "I'm sorry. We've had car trouble. It's fixed now, and we'll be on our way."

"Don't mean to be unfriendly," the man said. "But you can't be too careful nowadays."

"Ain't that the truth?" Mari smiled and motioned for the others to get in the Suburban.

"Nice country bumpkin act," Brad said as he slid behind the wheel.

"Acting is part of the job." There wasn't any part of Mari's past career choice that she did like. Not anymore.

Ten years off in La-La land had done a complete turnaround in her moral structure. Not that she faulted Brad for his job choice. The man was good at what he did and seemed to do so with as much integrity as possible. Mari could only hope she'd been as good.

"Why aren't they leaving?" Jeanna peered between the front seats. "You don't think they're bad guys, do you?"

Mari's blood ran cold. The man and woman were back in the truck, but instead of backing out so Brad could drive back to the highway, they sat and stared. "Can you get around them?"

"I can try." Brad turned the key in the ignition, gave the wheel a sharp turn, and spun gravel squeezing past the older model truck. Tree branches scraped the sides of the Suburban. The couple in the truck turned to watch as they moved past. "If they follow us, we'll know they aren't just a friendly couple out to protect their land."

The beat-up truck pulled onto the road behind them. Brad increased his speed while Mari turned and kept watch out the back window. The rust stains and dents in the truck's body were deceiving. A powerful engine hid under the hood. The faster they went, the faster the truck went.

"Why can't we catch a break?" Mari pounded the back of the seat. "We can't head to the safe house until we lose them."

"I'll lose them. Make sure your seatbelts are fastened and trays in their upright positions." Brad stomped the gas and sent them rocketing down the highway.

Mari braced herself against the dashboard and kept watch out the back window, expecting to see the barrel of a shotgun at any minute, and prayed they wouldn't have an accident. She didn't relish going through the front windshield. Dad turned in his seat, shotgun propped on the headrest. She smiled at his gumption. He'd do anything to protect his girls.

Her smile faded at the frightened look on her daughter's face. Twelve was too young for the life she'd been asked to live. Somehow, Mari would make it up to her daughter. To her parents, too. There had to be a home with a white picket fence somewhere in Mari's future. She planned on finding it.

~

Brad kept a tight grip on the steering wheel. Their pursuers didn't seem concerned about shooting, only staying on their tail as if he and the others were cattle to be herded. He eased up on the gas.

"What are you doing?" Mari shot him a sharp glance.

"They're sending us where they want us to go. Hang on." He whipped the steering wheel until they raced in the opposite direction. They sped past the truck, leaving the occupants with open mouths and wide eyes. Good. He hoped the truck didn't have the turning radius the company vehicle did. "Now, we'll lose them."

The truck had just switched direction when Brad rounded a curve on the highway. He took an access road and sped west. It would take a few extra hours this way, but hopefully those chasing them wouldn't think to get off the highway.

Mari and Dan shifted back to sitting positions and fastened their seatbelts. "That was brilliant." Mari flashed Brad a smile that sent his heart into overdrive.

Maybe he should've let Nichols assign someone else to the case. It wouldn't be beneficial for Brad to have romantic feelings toward the woman he was assigned to protect. But no, he didn't want anyone else to be responsible for bringing Tom's killers to justice. He'd have to work harder on keeping his emotions neutral toward the beautiful woman next to him.

"I'm sick of driving and running." Mari propped her feet on the dashboard.

"I'm hoping we can have some peace once we get to my friend's cabin."

"Not the safe house?"

"No." Not if the agency had a possible mole.

"So, no one will know where we are?"

"Only one person. My boss."

"You trust him?"

"With my life." What would Brad do if Hoover showed

up at Ryan's cabin? He couldn't imagine Nichols betraying one of his men. Why use a valuable man to babysit her? It all boiled down to the list stored in her head.

When there was no further sign of the rednecks in the battered truck, Brad relaxed his hold on the wheel. The further north they drove, the thicker the trees and the lower the temperature. What if he was making a mistake? What if Ryan's cabin turned out to be nothing more than a trap? They could have taken a place in the city, but that might put innocent people at risk. He would have to trust that he'd made the right decision.

Dusk had settled over the mountain like a well-worn quilt by the time he turned down the little-used road to the cabin. His passengers slept. Brad yawned. Too many sleepless nights for him, and there were plenty more to come. The thought alone smothered him with exhaustion.

"I'll take first watch tonight." Mari's soft words drifted across the space between their seats.

"It's my job."

"You can't do a good job if you're dead on your feet." She straightened and rotated her head on her shoulders. "I'm rested. Let me take the watch. Stop being a hero."

He wanted to protest again, but she was right. He'd be of no use to anyone if he didn't get some rest. "Fine."

"And I'll take second," Dan said. "This way, you can get at least six hours."

Brad chuckled. "I get the hint. I'm not in this alone."

"Darn right." Dan gave a nod and crossed his arms. "Get used to accepting help when it's offered. It makes it easier on all of us."

Thirty minutes later, he stopped in front of a thousand square foot cabin. When Ryan died in the line of duty a year ago, taken down by two shots in the chest, he'd Willed the cabin to Brad. He'd only come up once and that was right after the funeral. Inside was one bedroom and a loft. A small kitchen tucked in the far corner of the open room, a fireplace that took up one whole wall, and some comfortable but well-worn furniture. The best place about the cabin was the log walls. It would be hard for a bullet to pierce through.

"I left the place well-stocked when I was here last. With what you guys managed to bring, we should be okay for a week before we need to make a run into town," he said.

Dan glanced at the pewter sky. "Looks like snow this far up."

"Wouldn't be unheard of." Brad shivered in his tee shirt. "Let's get unloaded, and I'll get a fire started."

"Start the fire and we'll do this," Mari said, her teeth chattering.

Brad loped to the cabin and unlocked the door. He left it open for ease of the others going in and out, and reached above the fireplace mantel for the matches. Soon, crimson flames licked at the wood. He stretched his hands over the warmth. It was getting cold fast, and the fireplace was the only source of heat other than the kitchen stove. They might not be using the loft after all. His guess was everyone would hunker down to sleep in front of the fire for safety's sake.

"Wow, what a difference a thousand feet of elevation makes." Mari set a box on the handmade wood table. "It feels more like winter than fall."

"Snow could be our friend." Brad stood and turned his back to the fire. "Footprints would stand out, and it's hard to hide against a white landscape."

"True, but snow is also blinding." She started unpacking the box and placing food items on a high shelf. "I think I had a job once where I was in the snow. The image seems pretty vivid. I can almost feel the pain of it in my eyes."

"Good. You're remembering more every day." He left the warmth of the fire and helped her unpack. Maybe by the time they were discovered, she would have remembered everything.

CHAPTER SIXTEEN

The sun hadn't risen yet when Mari woke. The light from the fireplace illuminated Brad sitting in front of the door. His shoulders were slumped, his head hanging, his hands dangling between his knees. She crawled out of her sleeping bag and made her way to his side. "Do you want some coffee?"

The face he turned to her ripped at her heart. Sadness pulled at the corners of his mouth. Every line showed dejection.

She placed a hand on his shoulder. "What's wrong?"

"Nothing. I'm fine." He shrugged her off and stared out the window.

"I'm a good listener. Let me fix the coffee while you decide whether you want to talk." She shoved aside the way his cold shoulder was like a punch in the gut. They were partners now. If something bothered him, it bothered her.

She filled the glass pot with water and measured grounds into the filter. Who was she kidding? She didn't know when she'd stopped looking at him as just a partner, but he meant more. Now might not be the time for romantic entanglements, but for once, her heart softened toward a man who wasn't an assignment. Brad wasn't someone she was paid to pretend to love.

Her hand shook as she pressed the button on the coffee maker. Love. Did she even know what real love toward a man was like? Other than what she saw between her parents, she had no idea of true affection between a man and a woman. Maybe she'd loved Jeanna's father, but since she couldn't remember his name, or his face, how could she know?

The deep aroma of brewing coffee filled the cabin. Brad joined her in the kitchen area and plopped into a chair. She turned, ready to ask him to talk. The strain on his face dissolved her question. Instead, she busied her hands pulling down blue metal mugs speckled with white.

Once the coffee was done, she poured it into the mugs and handed him one before sitting next to him. Her hand shook as she placed it over his. When he didn't pull away, she threaded her fingers with his. "We're partners, Brad. I'm not just your assignment. I want to remember as much as you want me to. I want to keep my family safe as much as you do."

"I failed to keep Tom safe, I dated a killer, what if I fail now?" He raised red-rimmed eyes to hers.

"I failed your brother." Her throat clogged. "That wasn't you."

He smirked and looked away. "I blamed you at first, but not anymore. There wasn't anything you could have done."

"You need to listen to your words." She lifted her drink, keeping her right hand entwined with his, and sipped the black drink, the rich acidic taste rolling past her tongue. "We can't save everyone. I'm just sorry your brother was one we lost." She squeezed his hand. "We won't lose anyone under this roof. We won't."

He sighed. "I'm tired, I guess. My mind is running in circles trying to figure out the mole in the agency."

"You didn't sleep?"

"I did for about five hours. It was glorious." He grinned, deep dimples winking from his cheeks. "Now, the inactivity of waiting will make me insane."

"We can relieve a bit of that boredom." Dan approached them, Jeanna's wood keepsake box in his hand. "This has a false bottom. I think you'll be happy with what's in it."

"The list?" Mari set her mug down and grabbed the box. In the corner of the bottom was a small indentation. She pressed it. A secret drawer popped out. Inside, nestled on a strip of black velvet, was a computer jump drive. "I wonder if I put the assassination ring's names on it."

"Let's check." Brad took the drive from her. "The vehicle outside has a d in the center console. Dan, for your protection, you can't see this."

He nodded. "I'll wait here and have my morning java. Good luck."

Mari dashed after Brad, who sprinted for the Suburban. He pressed some buttons and the console opened, revealing a small laptop. "So James Bond-ish," she said.

"There are a few perks to the job." He slid the drive into the port. Names scrolled across the screen. "These are the agents. There…" He pointed at a second list, typed in a different font. "These are the assassins." He beamed up at Mari from the driver's seat. "Good job, Lu Lu."

"So, it's over?" Her heart leaped.

"No," he said, dashing her hopes. "We have to get this to Nichols and bring down Hoover and his buddies who want you dead. Then it will be over."

She'd so hoped life could regain some semblance of normalcy upon finding the list. "I guess they would be upset that I infiltrated their ring. I made them look stupid." She leaned against the vehicle. "So, now what? We draw them out? I don't want my family involved in a gun fight, and I don't think just the two of us can take them on our own."

He slid from the vehicle. "I'll have to do some thinking." He slid the drive into his pocket.

"We," Mari wagged her finger from him to her, "need to do some thinking. Team, remember?"

He laughed, the sound deep and rumbling like a summer thunderstorm. "I'm sure you'll keep reminding me." He slung an arm around her shoulders. "Come on, partner, it's cold out here."

Maybe to him. His arm around her sent lava flowing through Mari's veins. It didn't help to cool her off, either, when he gave her a squeeze at the door before releasing her and ushering her in ahead of him.

~

Mari smelled like citrus and flowers. Brad released her and took another whiff before she headed into the house. The glow on her face upon finding the jump drive kept his heart in overdrive. Maybe it was the actual finding of what they sought, but he doubted it. No, his new "partner" was dangerous to his senses.

"Any luck?" Dan glanced up from the kitchen table where he sat with Jeanna. Mary Ellen fried bacon on the ancient propane stove.

Brad nodded. "Exactly what we wanted. Now, to find a way of getting it to my boss."

Dan handed him another drive. "Maybe you should copy the files on this first."

"Good idea." Brad had planned on heading into town to get another drive, now he could stay where he was really needed. He looked at the faces around the table: the child, the couple, the woman he was growing to care too much for as the pressure to protect increased. With one false move, an entire family could be wiped out. He couldn't let that happen. He'd never be able to live with himself.

He pushed up from the table and took his duffel bag onto the front porch. Cold or not, he wanted to make sure his weapons were cleaned and loaded. Hoover *would* show up. Somehow he'd find out where they were, and Brad would not be caught off guard.

The door opened and closed behind him. He caught Mari's fragrance before she sat on the stoop next to him. Without speaking, she took a high-powered rifle from the bag and started to clean it. Did it occur to her that she picked up some of her old talents without seeming to think about them?

Maybe a few days of relaxation without someone trying to kill them will allow her mind to rest and remember. Not that it was as important as before, except for Mari's peace of mind. They had what they needed.

Brad couldn't imagine how awful it would be to not know your past, though. He watched as she disassembled and reassembled with skill and speed, then lifted the rifle to peer down the barrel.

"Done that much?" He bumped her with his shoulder.

She laughed. "A little it seems like. Funny how so much comes back to me when I start doing the work." She rested the rifle in her lap. "How will we spend the days here? No television, no phones, no radio … we've been stuck in the past without the livestock and hunting to do."

"Oh, we'll be hunting." He grinned. "These woods could be full of possible predators."

"I presume you mean the two-legged kind."

"Is there any other?" He sat a Glock into the bag. "I want to set a few traps. If they do find us, they won't sneak up on us, not if I can help it. I also need to call my boss." What kind of code could he use to let Nichols know he'd found the drive without alerting any eavesdroppers? He also wanted the evidence out of his hands as soon as possible.

He pulled his phone from his pocket and walked around the corner of the house. When Nichols answered, he said, "Don't let on that it's me."

"Hey, sweetheart. We had to call an exterminator." Nichols's deep voice vibrated over the airwaves. "Not sure we got all the little buggers."

"I have a particular little beast of my own. It's like a

disease I can't wait to pass on."

"Hmmm. Interesting. Remember that place we went on our first date?"

Brad grinned. The first time he'd had lunch with his boss, they'd gone for Chicago-style hot dogs. He wasn't sure the nearest town had one, but he'd be willing to bet any hot dog place would work. "Do you mind if we buy extras?"

"Not at all. Lunch time tomorrow." Click.

Brad headed for the laptop in the Suburban. Inside, door closed against the chill, he did a Google search for hot dog restaurants. There were two. One in the town of Hoppersville, ten miles away, and another in Morris Town which was farther, but still only fifteen miles. Morris as in his last name Morrison.

He hoped his gamble would pay off. After copying the information onto the spare jump drive Dan had given him, he opened the door and marched back to the cabin, grabbing the duffel bag next to Mari on his way. "Come on, Lu Lu. We're all going to lunch."

"What?" She leaped to her feet and rushed after him.

"I have a lunch meeting tomorrow, and we're all going. It's best if we all stay together."

"I agree, but is it safe to leave here?"

Brad faced her. "We need to turn over the drive. It's safer if it isn't in our possession."

"You know that won't get John off our tail. He'll hound us until—"

"I know." They were dead. She didn't need to finish her sentence. Their lives would be in danger until John was out of the picture. "But that drive will have the name of the ring's leader on it, and my boss has resources we don't. Take out the chief and the tribe falls apart." He hoped.

Mari didn't look convinced. She chewed the inside of her cheek and kept her eyes focused on his. "You're sure this is the right thing to do? We won't have a bargaining chip if we hand it over."

"I copied the files." Still no guarantee, but it was all they had. He put his hands on her shoulders. "Trust me. I'm doing the best I can."

She nodded. "I do trust you. I'm sorry about the diner—"

"I know. You're worried and scared. Having your family here doesn't help." Despite his resolve to keep his distance, he pulled her close and leaned her head against his chest. *God, let him be able to protect this woman and her family.*

CHAPTER SEVENTEEN

Mari spotted the large black man the moment she stepped out of the Suburban. She grinned and increased her pace, shoving open the glass door to Morris Town's Hot Dog Haven. "Eight Ball!"

Nichols grinned. "You remember me."

"The moment I laid eyes on your handsome face." She stepped into his hug, breathing in his familiar scent of Polo cologne. "Thank you for watching out for my family while I … was gone."

"It was my pleasure. You ready to come back to work?" He set her at arm's length, his dark gaze roaming across her face.

She shook her head. "Consider this my resignation."

"You want the picket fence life now?" His brow furrowed. "One of my best agents throwing in the towel?"

"That's exactly what I want." No more killing, even in the line of duty, for her.

"Morrison." Nichols reached around her and shook Brad's hand.

Mari didn't miss the subtle exchange of the jump drive, or the quick drop into Nichols's pocket. She glanced around the small diner. No one seemed to be paying them undue attention. Still, the back of her neck prickled. "We need to sit." She headed to a corner booth away from the windows.

Once they were seated, Nichols ordered hot dogs and fries for everyone. Jeanna stared at the basket the hot dog sat in. "I don't like hot dogs."

Mari bit back a laugh. "These are supposed to be good ones."

"I'll try it, but no promises." She took a deep breath and brought her lunch to her mouth. "I wish you guys would catch those people chasing us so life can get back to normal."

They all laughed, except Jeanna, who glared while taking a bite of her food. While her behavior was funny, Mari agreed. She wasn't sure what "normal" was in regards to her life, but she wanted something traditional: a husband, more children, a house in the country.

She met Brad's warm gaze. He winked, sending her blood pressure soaring and her mind dwelling on forbidden what ifs. She picked up her food and started to eat. The first bite reminded her that she, too, didn't care for hot dogs. What else did she have in common with her daughter? God willing, she'd have many years to find out.

"Are you sure you weren't followed?" Brad asked Nichols.

"Yes. I don't have a GPS on my vehicle. It isn't needed. All the bugs seem to be gone from my office. I think the IT guy, Skip Hastings, is the mole. He hasn't shown up for work since you visited the office." He shook his head. "I just can't believe one of our own would turn on a fellow agent, but it all makes sense. He has access to all records and files. Has the address to every safe house, and keeps tabs on agents via GPS."

"It happens. Look at Sarah." Brad tossed his napkin on the table. "I sure didn't see that one coming."

The food in Mari's stomach soured. How could she eat

with the vision of Sarah on the bathroom floor with a bullet in her head that Mari put there? She shoved aside her basket. "We should go." She pushed to her feet. "It was great seeing you again, Eight Ball. I wish it were under better circumstances."

"Why do you call him Eight Ball?" Jeanna asked.

"Because my head is black and shiny like the eight ball in pool, little miss." Nichols stood. "Keep in touch daily. I need to know y'all are okay."

"We will," Brad said. "You be careful, too."

Mari glanced over her shoulder as they left the diner. The expression on Nichols's face looked like he thought he'd never see them again. Which could be very true. They'd taken a huge risk heading into town, and she couldn't shake the feeling they were under surveillance.

Brad must have had the same feeling. He ushered the family inside the Suburban and scanned the parking lot. Nichols watched from inside the diner. When no one confronted them, Brad slid behind the wheel and tossed Mari a look of reassurance. She smiled and settled back in her seat, trying to ignore the niggling sensation of being watched without seeming worried.

There was no way John could know where they were. Not without GPS on Brad's phone and on the truck. She wracked her brain trying to think of another way they could be traced. Her heart stopped. "Mom, have I always had a mole on my upper right shoulder?"

"No, why?"

Mari shot Brad a look. "Must be sun damage." She was the reason her family was in constant danger of being killed. The minute they returned to the cabin, she'd have Brad dig it out of her and destroy the chip. She hoped she'd get a chance to personally strangle John for the torment they were all forced to endure.

The drive back to the cabin was silent. Jeanna had ear buds in her ears and listened to an ipod. Mom and Dad stared out the window. Brad focused on the road. Mari knew they weren't, but everyone seemed at peace. Maybe they were just resigned to their fate and the fact that the real trouble was yet to come.

A war was fast approaching, one Mari wasn't sure they could win. She spent the rest of the drive up the mountain in prayer.

As soon as the vehicle stopped a few feet from the front door, she slid out and rushed into the house and into the bathroom. Inside, she slammed the door and yanked off her thick jacket and then her shirt. There. A raised black mole she thought she'd had her whole life. She twisted, trying to get a better look.

"Mari?" Brad knocked on the door. "I'm coming in."

She sighed. So what if he'd see her in her bra. There were more important things at stake than modesty. "Come on."

To his credit, Brad's eyes widened, then immediately turned away. In his hand, he held a small knife the size of a scalpel. "Turn around. This is going to hurt."

"I can handle it." She turned and closed her eyes. She hissed as the knife cut into her skin.

"Sorry."

"Hurry."

"You do know it won't make any difference, right?" Brad cut deeper. "They already know where we are."

~

His gut clenched with each dig of the knife. The mole on her back was a lump someone had tattooed black. Obvious to anyone bothering to look that it was man made, but excellently done to a casual observer. No time for regrets. The damage was done.

"There." He reached over her shoulder and showed her the small silver disc. "Do you want the honors?"

She took the tracking device, ground it under her foot, then flushed the pieces down the toilet. "Can you stitch me?"

"Sorry. No needle and thread for this sort of thing, but there are butterfly band aids in the medicine cabinet." He retrieved them and set to work patching her up.

His hands still trembled a bit from the sight of her in a black lacy bra. Her skin was warm under his touch and the intoxicating scent she wore teased his senses. He wanted nothing more than to pull her into his arms and kiss her until she was as senseless as he.

His face in the mirror must have reflected his thoughts. Mari met his gaze and held it, holding her breath. For several long seconds they stared at each other. Brad shook off his desires. "You're all set." He dashed from the room as if chased by angry bees.

In the kitchen, he washed his hands in the sink and leaned, palms and head down, against the counter. He'd come so close to blowing it all. Admitting his feelings for her would jeopardize everything.

"My girl taken care of?" Dan approached and turned on the coffee pot.

"Yeah. She had a chip." Brad steeled his features into impassiveness. "We can expect company soon."

"Need help with those traps I heard you telling Mari about?"

"Yes." The older man's help would be appreciated and, with his skills as a hunter, invaluable. "There should be some empty film cartridges in a box under the back seat of the Suburban. I'll get a box of shotgun shells."

"Making land mines?"

"That and other stuff." He shouldn't be surprised that Dan would know of simple items used for booby traps, but he was. "I'd dig a pit if we had time." Brad opened the cabinet under the kitchen sink and pulled out a box of shells and another of nails. If anyone stepped on any of their surprises planted around the perimeter, walking would be very difficult.

"I can set trip wires." Mari leaned against the table, her

117

Glock in the waistband of her jeans. "If someone trips it, they'll get a couple of nasty spikes in the neck."

"Who are you guys?" Jeanna stared with wide eyes from the living room sofa. "It's like I've walked into a Rambo movie or something."

"You pretty much have, sweetheart." Mari strolled over and ruffled her daughter's hair.

Jeanna grimaced. "I'm a little too old for that, Mari."

No one could miss the look of pain that crossed Mari's face, or the intention behind Jeanna's words. If her mother had been around, she'd know Jeanna was too old for those types of affection.

Mary Ellen agreed to stay in the cabin, doors locked, with Jeanna, while the other three secured the perimeter. They put together the mines, then set out in three directions about fifty yards from the cabin. With the abundance of fallen leaves, hiding the mines wasn't difficult. Once that was done, the men set to work whittling stakes while Mari stretched a thin line of fishing wire around the area inside the circle of mines.

It wasn't much, might not be enough to stave off a gun fight, but it was all they had. That, and their weapons. Brad glanced at the sky. There'd be snow by morning. At least the weather was on their side.

Mary Ellen opened the door upon their return. "I made cookies." She shrugged. "I had to keep busy. Jeanna's been practicing loading the guns."

"No way." Mari planted fists on her hips and frowned. "She's too young. She'll stay out of the way if it comes to shooting."

"Puh-leese." Jeanna shoved past her, a cookie in her hand. "I've been shooting since I was five. Grandma doesn't intend for me to shoot, only to keep the weapons loaded. Seriously. You've been gone my whole life. What right do you have to play mother hen now?"

Mari paled. "You're right. I apologize." She headed to

the back of the cabin and into the bedroom.

"That was rude and uncalled for." Mary Ellen glowered and snatched the cookie from Jeanna's hand. "I think you should spend some time in the loft thinking over what you said."

"Whatever." Jeanna climbed the ladder and disappeared.

While Brad was grateful for another person with a knowledge of guns, he wished to be anywhere but there. He tried to busy himself looking for … something in the cupboards. Anything to make him look busy and to keep attention away from him. The low murmurs of Dan and Mary Ellen told him they were most likely discussing how to handle their hurting pre-teen.

Brad was more interested in the hurting woman in the bedroom. Forgetting her daughter wasn't Mari's fault. Yes, she signed over her rights as guardian, but until the amnesia, there were no rules against seeing family members. He'd visited his parents on a regular basis until their deaths a few years ago.

"Sorry about the display of bad behavior." Mary Ellen slammed a pot onto the stove. "That girl knows better."

"No apology necessary." Brad grabbed cans of soup. "Supper?"

"Perfect." She motioned for him to set them on the counter. "I'm glad my girl is quitting your line of business. My old heart can't take the danger anymore. Maybe once this is all over, she'll be able to repair what was broken with her own daughter."

"I hope so." Brad glanced out the window as the first snowflakes started to fall. "All of you are holding up remarkably well."

"We don't really have a choice, do we?" She cut him a sideways glance as she dumped chicken noodle soup into the pan. "We knew what could happen when we entered the witness protection after believing Marilu dead. God brought her back to us, He'll get us out of this."

CHAPTER EIGHTEEN

Mari perched on the edge of the sagging mattress. Jeanna was right. Mari didn't have the rights of a parent. She couldn't tell her daughter what to do.

Tears burned her eyes. She blinked them away and stared out the window at the falling snow. If the snow fell too heavily, their homemade bombs wouldn't work. Wait. They'd set most of them along the tree line. Hopefully, the thick pine branches would prevent the snow from covering the mines.

A sob tore at her throat. Here she sat, saddened by her daughter's rebuff, and instead of lamenting her loss, she worried over traps that could maim or kill another human. This was who she was. Not the doting mother or caring daughter. She was an agent trained to kill. She covered her face. What was wrong with her?

"Mari?" Mary Ellen rapped at the door. "I'm bringing you some soup."

"I'm not hungry." Feeling as young as her daughter, Mari flopped back onto the bed.

"I'm bringing it in anyway." Her mother pushed the door open and set a tray on the nightstand. "Oh, honey.

Don't let Jeanna's words wound you. She's confused."

"I'm not upset about that." Mari laid her arm across her eyes. "Instead of thinking about how I can improve my relationship with her, I'm thinking of how much the snow could mess up the traps we laid. I'm an evil person."

Mom laughed. "No, you're not." The mattress bent under her weight. "It's hard to let go of a lifetime of habit, and your habits have lain dormant for a long time. They're just now making themselves known."

"I hate who I am." Tears ran down her cheeks and into her hair.

"I think you should have asked Nichols to give you a copy of your employment file." Mom patted her shoulder. "My guess is that you've saved a lot more people than not."

"How?" Mari shot to a sitting position. "Tom Morrison was my first assignment. I let him die."

"He was the first assignment you were assigned to kill undercover of the assassination ring. You were also assigned to protect him. Don't forget you worked undercover. The memories will return, and you'll see that before infiltrating the ring, you succeeded many times. I know it."

"How do you know?" Mari searched her face for the truth in her words.

Mom placed a hand over her heart. "I know it in here." She moved her hand to her head. "And in here. Ask Brad. I bet he knows a lot about you."

Why couldn't her memories return without questions? Maybe she didn't like the fact that Brad probably knew more about her than she did. It seemed intimate somehow, and that was a feeling she wasn't ready to explore. She wasn't sure she would ever be ready. In her mixed up brain, she'd been married twice, both false marriages, it turned out.

Mom left the soup and two thick slices of bread. Mari's stomach rumbled, and she grabbed one of the slices spread thick with butter. If she ate slow, she could prolong the time until she had to face the others.

As the snow fell outside, the room grew colder, until Mari was forced to go into the main part of the house heated by the massive fireplace. Her father and daughter played a game of checkers, while her mother sat curled up with an afghan, a cup of something hot in her hand. Brad stood in front of the large window. Everyone but he and Jeanna greeted her with a smile. Jeanna avoided her gaze, keeping her focus on the game.

Mari shrugged. Her daughter would or would not accept her in time. Mari could do nothing at this point, except love her and try to keep her safe.

A loud snap sounded and the lights went out. "Tree branch fell on the electrical wires," Brad said. "It's candles and lanterns for now."

They didn't need them with the fire's blaze, but Mari needed something to occupy her hands. "Where are they?"

"A drawer in the kitchen. Matches, too."

The fire's glow didn't reach as far as the kitchen and Mari searched dark drawers until she found what she wanted" a box of utilitarian white candles and a box of matches. She'd spotted candlesticks on the mantel earlier and set two of the candles in the holders. They were ready if needed. Now she sat on the opposite end of the sofa with nothing to do.

She might as well try to figure out what John would do. After all, she'd been "married" to him for ten years. First, he'd definitely come after her. He'd guess that she'd make a copy of the drive once she found it. Second, he wouldn't come alone. She had no idea who he worked with, but he'd bring backup. Third, he wouldn't kill her outright. He'd try to take her somehow, make her pay for the inconvenience of chasing her.

Early in their fake marriage, he'd been violent, hitting her when she didn't conform fast enough to his idea of the ideal wife. Once he'd set the alarm on the house, locking her inside with threats of more violence if she triggered the alarm to escape. Not once had he told her the code to disarm the alarm. Acid churned her stomach. Their entire farce of a wedding had become day after day of physical and mental torture.

The memories slammed into her like a mudslide. For ten years he'd punished her for infiltrating a secret association and showing him to be a fool. She'd bested him once, she could win again.

~

The big windows left them exposed. Anyone with binoculars could see them playing games, eating, passing the time. Brad had seen sheets of plywood somewhere. The back of the house. "Dan, cover me out the back door. We should cover the windows."

Dan grabbed his shotgun from where he had propped it next to the front door. "I'm on it."

Brad hurried out the back door to the wood pile. Five sheets of plywood, a saw, and an ax. He left the ax stuck in a chunk of firewood and grabbed the largest sheet he could find. Ryan had used these when he'd close up the cabin on the off months. After his death, no one bothered, and Brad hadn't thought of it the last time he'd been there.

After nailing the wood over the front window, he cut two holes big enough for the barrel of a gun and for a person to see through. Dan started on a sheet for the bedroom, while Brad moved to the small kitchen window. He thought he saw movement in the thick pines. Surely not even Hoover would brave the outdoors on a night such as this one. His eyes were playing tricks.

The boards shut out the glisten of the falling snow and cast the room further into darkness. Even daytime would be dark. Although they were better protected, the closing off of the windows left Brad uneasy. Unless a trap was triggered, they'd have little advance warning of an attack.

"There's a window in the loft," Jeanna said. "More like a porthole, actually."

Their one good vantage point, and it faced the back of the house. Brad scampered up the ladder. Across from the loft, another small circle of glass taunted him, useless. They had no way of getting an unobstructed view of the front of the house. He'd have to make a bigger hole in the plywood.

There was no suspense in wondering whether Hoover and his buddies would arrive, they would come with evil intent. The question was when. Would they wait for the snow to stop completely, or use its cover to hide their approach? Time was of the essence. Brad rushed back down the ladder and took the saw in his hand.

After the others bedded down for the night in front of the fireplace, Brad stood in front of the hole in the board. The hole was big enough for his face and nothing more, but it did increase his line of vision.

Mari stepped to his side. "It's still coming down pretty hard out there."

"That's a good thing." Unless it snowed enough to allow someone access to the window in the loft. "You can't sleep?"

She shook her head, sending silky strands of hair kissing his face. He curled his fingers into a fist to keep from running them through her hair. The firelight cast half her face in the shadow, the other half was highlighted with silver from the meager light coming through the slit in the board. She was ethereal, a beautiful maiden from another world.

His gaze dropped to her full lips. They weren't alone in the dark, but they might as well be. She stared into his eyes. Her tongue flicked across her lips, sending his pulse racing. *Say something, you idiot!* What was it about this woman that tied his tongue in a knot?

"Tell me about myself." Her whispered question cut through the thick mud of his brain.

"You're Marilu Suzette Hutchins, age thirty-five, daughter of – "

"No." She shook her head, sending her hair flying

again. With a huff, she shoved it behind her ears. "I'm sure you've read my file. Tell me what it says."

"Okay." He ran his hands through his hair. The gesture most likely made him look like a porcupine. "You're an agent with Agency for the Protection of Civilians. APC."

"A bodyguard?"

"For hire. We guarded people with government secrets or on asylum from the Middle East and European countries. You were very good at your job, according to your file."

"How many people did I fail to protect?"

He wanted to lie and tell her none, but couldn't. "You protected more than twenty people in your short career."

"Was Tom the only one I failed?" She gripped the front of his shirt.

"Yes."

"You must hate me." She pulled away.

He took her hands in his and forced her to look at him. "No. You didn't kill my brother. Sarah and someone else did. I don't blame you."

"But you did when you thought I'd crossed to the other side."

"Yes. I was wrong. You're assignment with my brother and the assassination ring was on a need to know basis. Nichols didn't think I needed to know." That knowledge hurt, knowing that Nichols didn't think him strong enough to keep quiet when his brother was in danger. Still, he wouldn't have been any better of a protector against an unseen sniper than Mari had been. It wasn't her fault.

She turned, keeping one of her soft hands in his. She leaned close and laid her head on his shoulder. "I remember now. Most of the people I was assigned to were women. Because Tom knew about the ring is why I was assigned to him, and I still haven't figured out why I was with Jack. Maybe it will come to me and maybe it won't. I was able to keep an eye on Tom for APC and still pretend to keep tabs on John's ring. That was easily my most difficult assignment, until now."

"You aren't working."

"Yes, I am. I'm helping you keep my family safe, and I'll do whatever it takes."

"So will I." He laid his cheek against her soft head.

"I know you will."

They stood like that, wrapped in each other's arms, taking comfort in a common goal while the snow continued to pile up outside. For a moment, Brad could almost forget why they were there and look on the evening as a romantic getaway with a beautiful woman. Until her father's snores brought him back to reality.

They weren't on vacation or a romantic rendezvous. They were waiting for a group of killers to arrive on their doorstep.

CHAPTER NINETEEN

Mari stirred scrambled eggs over the kitchen stove before the others woke, except her father, who took his turn at watch. She didn't know what time Brad had fallen asleep, but intended to let him sleep as long as he needed.

The snow outside had lessened to slowly falling flakes drifting past the windows. Snowdrifts piled three feet high around the cabin. It would be much easier for John to get to them than it would for them to flee. Maybe she should leave on her own, confront him, draw him away from her family.

Brad would be beside himself. But the longer Mari thought about it, the more sense it made. It was her John wanted anyway. The others didn't deserve to be killed because of her. She was expendable. Jeanna had her whole life ahead of her, with Mari's parents, the only guardians she'd ever known.

The coffee finished percolating, and she poured her father a cup, taking it to him. "You seem deep in thought this morning," he said.

"A lot on my mind." She stared out the small cut in the board. "They'll come soon. If not today, then tomorrow."

"We're ready for them."

She shook her head. "Me and Brad against several trained killers? It won't work. We'll all die."

"What am I? A spring chicken? Have you forgotten my military background?"

She had. Her father was trained military police. Still, she couldn't endanger his life.

"You can get that thought out of your head this minute." Dad pointed at her with his cup. "You're not going anywhere. We're in this together. Your mother and I lost you once, we don't plan on it happening again."

"But, Dad—"

"No, buts. We stay together." He turned back to watching out the window. "The eggs are burning."

Mari rushed back to the stove. Her father was wrong. She turned off the heat on the stove and popped slices of bread in the oven. Staying only prolonged the inevitable.

She watched as the others threw off their blankets and shuffled to the table. Everyone she loved resided under the wood-shingled roof. Even Brad. She smiled sadly at the blanket crease across his cheek and the way his hair stood up like a pin cushion. Several days of stubble darkened his jaw, making him even more attractive. Thoughts of what if flooded through her.

After breakfast, she'd find some excuse to go outside. Then, she'd take the truck and leave. They'd all be okay. Brad would tell Nichols they were stranded, and he would send someone for them.

She forced a smile to her face and set the cast iron skillet of eggs on the table, followed by another pan of bacon and the toast. She sat and glanced at the faces she loved, blinking back tears. Brad stared at her, his eyes narrowed. If she weren't careful, he'd figure out her plan and find a way to stop her.

It wasn't that she had a death wish, far from it. But leaving increased her family's chances of survival. She'd gladly make the sacrifice. "Anyone up for a game of checkers after breakfast?"

Brad still stared, his look darkening. "I thought I'd head out to check our traps."

Great. She couldn't leave with him outside.

"I thought maybe you could go with me," he told Mari, folding a slice of bacon in half and shoving it into his mouth.

He was on to her. Her shoulders slumped, and she nodded. "Of course."

Dad nodded and reached for the toast. "I think that's an excellent idea."

"Stool pigeon," Mari muttered under her breath.

"What was that, honey?" Dad raised his eyebrows, a glint in his blue eyes.

"Nothing." She pushed her eggs around on her plate with her fork and sighed. What was she, twelve, still letting her father tell her what to do? She met his gaze again, seeing the love there. Yes, after ten years away, she was once again Daddy's Little Girl. She didn't want to be anything else; that's why she wanted him safe.

He leaned across the table and laid his work-worn hand over hers. "I love you, sweetie."

"I know."

Jeanna seemed to watch them with curiosity written on her face. How would she feel if Mari were to disappear? She might feel abandoned again, but Mari still believed it would be in everyone's best interest if she left. Doing so now, when everyone was watching her, would be next to impossible.

After breakfast, while Mom and Jeanna washed the dishes, Mari bundled up in a warm coat, scarf and gloves, and followed Brad into the snow. They'd no sooner stepped around the corner when he whirled.

"What are you thinking? Leaving? Alone?" He threw his hands up and stormed a few feet away before marching back. "Do you know how stupid that sounds?"

"It makes perfect sense to me." Mari huddled down in

her coat. "John would leave the rest of you alone if he has me."

"You don't know that. We're loose ends, Mari." He gripped her shoulders. "He can't let any of us live. The only way out of this is to beat him."

"If he had me in custody, I could get close to him. I could finish him off."

He shook her, then released her. "That is the most insane idea I've ever heard."

She squared his shoulders. "He's going to take me anyway. Somehow, I'll be going with him. I only want to make sure the rest of you are safe."

"I won't let him have you." He grabbed her close, burying her face in the wool of his coat. "I'll die first."

Mari was afraid of that very thing.

~

"I'm doing my best!" Brad paced again. Couldn't she see that? If she were to leave, he'd have nothing to fight for. He stopped. Protecting Mari had stopped being just his job. He'd never survive if something happened to her.

"I know you are." Her eyes shimmered with unshed tears. "So am I. My family is the most important thing I have."

"Is that all?" His throat threatened to close, his heart to stop beating. "Are they the only people you care about?"

"No." He could barely hear her soft answer over the wind.

Dare he hope she was having the same feelings for him that he was having for her? He'd sworn after the fiasco with Sarah he'd never get involved with another woman from the agency, victim or protector. Now, here he was, his heart shattering at the thought that Mari wanted to leave and take her chances on her own.

He yanked her close, claiming her lips. The first touch was as cold as the frigid breeze that blew, but she quickly warmed, wrapping her arms around his neck and returning his kisses with a feverish fervor. Brad pushed her against the wall of the house, taking meager shelter under the eave, plastering his body over hers, not stopping to breathe, not stopping to think, consumed only with claiming her as his.

The cold and danger disappeared. He slipped his hands under the leather jacket she wore, skimming her ribcage and trying to pull her into himself. Their breathing quickened, their kisses deepened. He pulled free, nuzzling her neck, knowing what they were doing set them on a dangerous path, but not able to pull free.

Her hands slipped under his shirt. When had she removed her gloves? His flesh goose-pimpled from the breeze that accompanied them. They kissed from desire, they kissed knowing that, at that moment at least, they were alive, they kissed out of fear for the other.

"Stop." Mari pulled free. "This is insane."

"As crazy as you wanting to leave?" He nibbled her ear.

"Please." She ducked under his arm, her lips swollen from his kisses. "This isn't the time." She placed a hand against his heart. "God willing, we'll have time for this, but it isn't now."

She was right. He took a deep breath as she put her gloves back on. They couldn't afford the distraction. "You'll stay?"

"I'll stay." The sorrow on her face told him she still didn't agree it was the best thing to do. "I gather we didn't come out here to check the traps."

He chuckled. "No."

"Did you kiss me only to get me to agree to stay?"

"I had no intentions of doing anything but shake some sense into you." He stared into her eyes. "But I don't regret the kiss, just the timing. Do I owe you an apology?"

The corners of her mouth curled. "No. But we should head inside."

Brad grabbed her hand when she turned to leave. "We can't go back to the way things were."

"I know." She lowered her eyes. "I'm not sure I want to."

He definitely didn't. But their emerging feelings couldn't get in the way of his job. He scanned the tree line, worried they could have put themselves in danger while in the throes of passion. When all seemed clear, he led Mari back to the cabin and the warmth of the fire.

"Everything looks clear," he said, shedding his coat. "Snow has stopped though."

"I've got the weapons and ammo ready." Dan motioned toward the kitchen table. "We can handle a fight for a day, maybe two."

"We'll make every shot count." Brad glanced at the ceiling.

With several inches of snow around the perimeter and covering the roof, burning them out would be difficult. They had food and water for maybe a week. Plenty of time for Nichols to send help once they notified him of Hoover's arrival.

Brad had contemplated many times having Nichols send reinforcements before Hoover cornered them, but extra people would be hard to hide, and supplies would dwindle faster. Better to catch Hoover in the act. All Nichols would need was three hours to send help. They only needed to last that long.

He watched as Mari stood with her back to the fire. Her gaze met his, and she ducked her head, hiding behind her hair. He wanted to kiss her again and again. At that moment, resigning from the agency was no longer a question. Once Hoover was behind bars, he'd tell Nichols he wanted out. Then, he'd approach Mari about a future together. It would be easy enough for them to slip into the role of detectives within the police force or partner together as private investigators. He'd make sure she got the white picket fence life she craved.

The next hour was spent setting the weapons close to

every possible avenue of entrance to the cabin. Between himself, Dan, and Mari, they could cover both doors and the window, with Jeanna and Mary Ellen keeping their weapons loaded. Other than that, there was nothing to do but wait.

"Sun's out and it's blinding," Dan said. "No snow, sharp breeze, and it's beautiful. Too bad the beauty will allow the enemy to come."

Brad laughed. "Might want to wear your sunglasses, old man."

Dan patted his pocket. "Got 'em right here." He pulled them out and put them on. "Makes surveillance much easier. There's an extra pair on the table."

"Thanks." Brad slipped them on, resting them on top of his head. There didn't seem to be much the man hadn't thought of. He couldn't think of better people than him and Mari to do battle with.

Maybe they had a chance of walking away from it all. They were bunkered safe behind thick logs of wood, protected by high drifts of snow, with weapons and food. Brad had been in tougher situations and walked away.

As he reached for a cup of coffee, a small explosion sounded behind the cabin.

CHAPTER TWENTY

The first explosion froze Mari in place, the second sent her scrambling for her gun. As she grabbed the Glock and nearest rifle, her father and Brad also loaded themselves down with fire power while her mother and Jeanna sat on the floor with their backs against the wall. Mari's gaze met Brad's across the room. A split second of concern crossed his face before she headed for the back door.

Through the slit cut in the plywood over the window in the back door, Mari spotted a man running along the tree line. An explosion knocked him off his feet. Someone called out a warning to retreat. The injured man was left to crawl away on his own. Brad's idea worked, at least in slowing the attackers down.

John appeared in Mari's sight. He stared toward the house as if he could see her. She leveled her gun as he stepped back into the shadows, taunting her.

Mom knelt beside her. "I made coffee. It's going to be a long day and night."

"Thank you." Mari took the cup and set it on the counter next to her. "We're safe in here. They can't get to us."

"I'm not afraid. I have everything I need. My family, God, there isn't anything else." She patted Mari on the shoulder before taking coffee to the men.

Such simple faith, much like Mari's. But Mom remembered the past that brought her to God, Mari could only decipher fragments shifting inside her brain. Her gaze met the stern one of Brad's. He'd transferred from passionate to fiery, and not the romantic type of fire … the deadly kind.

He turned back to the boarded up window, leaving Mari feeling alone despite being surrounded by her family. She no longer wanted to leave on her own. She wanted them all to flee. But that was dangerous and ridiculous. They couldn't be on the run for the rest of their lives. No one could live that way. She should have pulled the trigger the instant John stepped from the protection of the trees.

The afternoon dragged by with no more explosions, no more sightings of John, and no signs of force. By early evening, Mari's eyes drooped and boredom threatened to suffocate her. She was almost tempted to run screaming across the snow and put a stop to the showdown.

Mom kept busy cooking and supplying them with something to drink. Jeanna sat on the sofa, a book in her hand. If Mari hazarded a guess, she'd say her daughter had yet to turn a page. She wasn't hysterical or weepy, just silent and withdrawn. Mari yearned to wrap her arms around her and promise everything would be okay. But that would be a lie, and her daughter wasn't open to hugs from a mother who hadn't raised her.

Mari closed her dry eyes. With nothing happening, maybe they could take turns resting, instead of the relentless eye strain of peering across a snow-covered lawn.

The jingle of a cell phone permeated the silence. Brad fished it from his pocket. "It's Nichols." He put the phone to his ear. "Tell me you're sending in the troops." He listened, the lines on his face deepening. After what seemed like endless minutes, he sighed and shoved the phone back in his pocket.

"The road up the mountain is slick with ice. They'll be here," he said. "But it will take a bit longer. Might not be until morning."

"Then how did John get here?" Mari rested the rifle on her knees.

"They must have been here before last night's freeze."

"Then where are they staying? They can't be living in the open. There has to be another cabin relatively close by."

Brad nodded. "I don't know where it is, though. Nichols will check satellite and see whether he can come up with something."

Mari wanted to ask whether Brad really trusted his boss. Maybe Sarah and the IT guy weren't the only traitors in the organization. Instead, she kept her mouth closed and stared out her narrow vantage point.

Knowing John was close left her unsettled. She wanted to hunt him down and put a stop to his threats. He wouldn't get the jump drive. She'd die keeping it from him. Maybe making a copy was a bad idea. If Nichols had the only copy, they could tell John they'd already handed it over.

Stupid. That wouldn't stop him. He wanted revenge for her leaving, for her infiltrating his ring, for turning over the drive, for a number of things. He wouldn't stop until he had her in his grasp again. Then, when he was done terrorizing her, he'd kill her, and possibly her family, too. She couldn't let the latter happen.

"Soup?" Mom handed her a bowl. "It's the best I could do for now."

Mari's stomach rumbled. Eating would at least relieve the boredom. She'd never been good with inactivity. Funny how she remembered mundane things at weird moments.

"We've got movement." Brad stiffened. "They're going to try and set fire to the house."

Mari set down her bowl and rushed to his side. Two men took cover behind the trees. Both carried torches. "Will it work?"

Brad shrugged. "I doubt it. The cabin is wet from the snow, but it could make a lot of smoke to cover their approach."

Her mouth dried. Her hand tightened on her rifle.

"Mari!" Jeanna pointed to the back door.

Someone was shoving a torch through the slit. Mari raced for the door, shoved the barrel of her rifle through the hole, and fired. A thud told her she'd hit her target. She turned and tossed the still burning torch into the sink.

A black scorched mark marred the wood floor where it had fallen. Mom dropped to her knees and scrubbed. It wouldn't help, but it gave her something to do. Mari didn't believe for a minute that her mother wasn't frightened of what their outcome could be. She hid it behind busyness.

Dad remained silent next to Brad, probably reliving the horror of his war days. What Mari wouldn't give to spare them all the next few hours. What she wouldn't do to prevent more bloodshed.

~

Brad had worried about Mari's ability to actually fire at someone, much less kill them after her behavior after killing Sarah. Now he knew she'd do what needed to be done and worry about her feelings later.

The torch shoved inside the cabin was a close call. He wanted to order that no one leaves their posts, but if the standoff lasted through the night, his request would be unreasonable. They'd have to take turns, having him or Dan guard the back if Mari needed a break.

He reached under his sunglasses and wiped a finger across his eyes, thankful for the protection against the sun's glare on the snow. As the sun set, the need for them would diminish, but his eyes would then strain to peer through the darkness. The moon would cast shadows that weren't there in the daytime, making it more difficult to determine what was real and what wasn't.

The men carrying torches and using sheets of metal as armor were very much real. "Incoming."

Dan aimed at their feet. His bullet kicked up snow. His second shot ricocheted off the metal with a sharp ping. "Those guys don't give up, do they?"

The two men approached the porch, then veered to the side of the cabin. Scampering overhead signaled their climb to the roof. "Get away from the fireplace, Jeanna."

She ducked behind the sofa as the first torch fell. Flames shot from the fireplace, igniting the sofa. She screamed and crawled backward. Mary Ellen rushed forward with a fire extinguisher. The second torch's fierce flames barely missed her.

"We can't do without the heat of the fire," she said. "Those torches must be doused in gasoline or something."

"We'll have to put the fire out and close the damper," Brad said. "Bundle up." He could only hope the roof didn't catch fire.

Clever trick, John Hoover. At least the occupants of the cabin were alert and not drowsing from boredom. "Jeanna, why don't you fill everything that will hold water?" It would keep the child busy and give them something to douse any fires Hoover was able to set. No fire would burn long with all the snow, but the man was proving to be inventive.

The girl rushed to do his bidding. A man who had snuck close while Brad was busy worrying about the fireplace, grabbed the end of Dan's gun. The man pulled, jerked down, then rammed the butt of the gun into Dan's chin. He fell like an oak tree.

"Dad!" Mari whirled.

"Don't leave your post." Brad glanced over his shoulder. "Mary Ellen, tend to your husband."

"I'm fine." Dan got to his feet. "Just clunked my teeth together. Surprised me is all. I'd like to see them try that stunt again."

They wouldn't. They'd come up with something else. So far, it was a game, but one Hoover would tire of quick enough. Brad needed to figure out what the man's next move would be. He hadn't a clue. He checked his watch. Nichols had called three hours ago. What was holding the man up?

A niggling of fear tickled the back of Brad's mind. Maybe his boss wasn't coming. Maybe he was as dirty as Sarah. Or, maybe something had happened as they tried to get to the cabin that would prevent them from coming. Ever.

The thought that Brad might be the sole protector of those in the cabin, that he may not be able to save them after all, churned his stomach. He'd been in worse situations, but those times he'd been with hardened military fighters.

An armored truck with a steel wedge-shaped bumper plowed through the snow and stopped a hundred feet from the cabin. The dome light came on, illuminating the face of John Hoover. The man leaned out his window, bullhorn in his hand. "Come on out, Stacy. Oh, I guess it's Marilu now, isn't it? Come out and spare the death of your family."

Mari stood next to Brad, her eyes wide in a pale face. Brad put a hand on her arm. "He won't stop even if you go out."

"I know." She leaned into him, putting her head on his shoulder.

"I think I can pick him off through the windshield," Dan said.

"I'm sure the glass is bullet proof," Brad said. "Save your ammo." He kissed the top of Mari's head. "You should go back. Hoover could be distracting us while someone comes to the back door. It's the weakest point in our defense."

She nodded and returned to her post. "Coast is clear."

Brad doubted it would stay that way.

Several minutes later proved him right. Men in bulky jackets, most likely covering Kevlar vests, surrounded the cabin in one big circle.

"You're outnumbered," Hoover called. "It's only a matter of time until we get in. Do you really want your family in that kind of danger?"

Jeanna ran into Mary Ellen's arms. "What are we going to do?"

"They can't stay out there all night," Dan said. "They'll freeze. We can wait until there are only a few and fight our way into the woods."

"It might come to that." Brad rolled his head on his shoulders. "We'll worry about that when, and if, the majority of these guys leave."

A boom sounded, then the cabin shook. Mari fired a shot. "They've got another vehicle ramming the cabin!"

"Cover me." Brad rushed up the ladder and to the loft window. Two men placed a ladder against the wall. Brad fired. They jumped out of sight. He was losing the battle. They couldn't win. They'd die here on the mountain.

"They've got axes." Mari shouted from below. "I can keep them from the back door, but only for so long."

"Do what you can." Brad climbed down from the loft and kicked over the ladder used as stairs.

"If you don't send Marilu out, I'll blow up the cabin."

Brad rushed to the window, Mari close at his side. Hoover stood next to a man with a military-issue Bazooka.

CHAPTER TWENTY-ONE

I t had finally come to her leaving. Mari handed her gun to Brad and shoved a small knife down her boot. John would make good on his threat, and he wouldn't give her long to make her decision.

"No. Absolutely not." Brad grabbed her arm. "We're all in this together."

"I cannot stand back and let my family be blown to bits." She slipped on her leather jacket. "If John wanted me dead, he had plenty of opportunities over the years." She cupped Brad's cheek and planted a soft kiss on his lips before meeting the shocked gazes of her family. She forced a shaky smile and reached for the door handle.

"Please, Mari, don't do this." Brad grabbed her to him, suffocating her. His fear radiated and threatened to dissolve her resolve.

She slipped from his arms and took a deep breath. With a quick prayer for deliverance, she opened the front door and stepped outside.

"It was almost too late," John said. "I've never been a patient man, as you well know."

Yes, she did. Every step closer to him felt like she was

headed to the gallows. Maybe she was. Her chances of seeing her family again, or the man she loved, were slim.

"No need to come any closer." John motioned for the man with the bazooka to keep it trained on the house. "Go get your daughter."

"No." The word tore at her throat. She couldn't. She took another step forward.

"If you don't, I'll fire on the house and they'll all die."

The tears she'd held back escaped and spilled down her cheeks. The cruel winter wind dried them to ice. As if on the verge of freezing herself, she turned and stiffly made her way back to the cabin.

Brad met her at the door. "What?"

"I have to take Jeanna with me." A sob choked off her words. She buried her face in his chest. "If I don't, he'll kill the rest of you."

"We've lived our life." Dad put an arm around us. "You don't have to do this."

She lifted her face. "I do. Jeanna has a chance, even if a small one, if she goes with me."

"I'll go." Jeanna grabbed her thick coat, then hugged each of her grandparents. "I'd rather take my chances than get blown up." She turned and slid her hand into Mari's, the gesture so sweet and trusting, that Mari's tears increased.

Mari glanced up at Brad. "Find us."

"With everything in me, I promise to get you free. Stay alive for me." He touched his forehead to hers.

She smiled. "I'll do my best." Giving her daughter's hand a squeeze, she headed back into the cold and toward evil.

Jeanna marched beside her, head held high, eyes on the man waiting for them. Pride in her daughter's courage filled Mari and gave her the strength to go forward. They'd find a way to get free. Brad would find them. God was with them.

"Happy now?" She faced John with as stern a look as she could muster. "Why do you need my daughter?"

"Leverage." John shoved Jeanna into the arms of a man standing beside him. "Let's get out of here before we freeze." He grabbed Mari by the arm and yanked her to his truck. After patting her down, missing the knife in her boot, John opened the back door. He shoved her inside and slid in beside her. Jeanna was put in a different vehicle.

Mari glanced out the window to see her baby's face pressed against the window, a gun to her head. She got the hint. No funny business or Jeanna would die. She crossed her arms and sat rigid against the back of the seat. Her fingers itched for the knife in her boot. She'd get her chance. All she needed to do was wait for the right moment.

"Why is it so important that you have me?" she asked. "We gave the information to Agent Morrison's supervisor."

"My poor naïve girl." Brad pinched her face between his fingers. "I don't believe for a minute that you didn't make a copy, nor do I believe that you didn't look at the information."

She didn't look at the information, but knew Brad had made a copy. A new drive was safely in Brad's pocket. She shrugged and pulled away from John, certain his grip would leave bruises. "Don't touch me. If you touch me again, I'll cut off those fingers."

A laugh burst from him, drawing attention from the driver. "You have never had the guts," John said. "Did you suddenly grow a backbone?"

"You have no idea," she muttered, then said louder, "What's so important about me anyway?"

John looked at her as if she were dense. "I invested ten years of my life in you. Why would I let you walk away?"

"You want me as your wife?" That made totally no sense and had to be the most insane thing she'd ever heard.

"Who said anything about a wife? But I did enjoy having a little woman around the house." He leered. "Since I needed to take you into captivity anyway, why not put you back in the role I modeled you for?"

"You'll never get away with it."

"I already have." He jerked a thumb toward the vehicle following them. "As long as that pretty little thing is in my clutches, you'll do anything I say. Welcome back to the world of assassination, Stacy Hoover."

Mari's heart dropped to her toes.

~

Brad tossed weapons into a duffel bag and grabbed his coat. He needed to get after Mari and Hoover as soon as possible.

"Where are you going to go?" Dan stopped him with a hand on his arm.

"I don't know." Brad sighed. "But their hiding place can't be far. There's no way they spent the night in frigid temperatures. I'll find them." He had to. He'd made a promise to Mari, and to his heart.

"I hope so." Dan put an arm around his wife. "We lost our daughter once, we don't want it to happen again. Now they have our granddaughter."

The roar of an engine reached his ears. Brad rushed outside to see Nichols climbing from a truck with snow chains on its tires. "You're too late. Hoover took Hutchins and her daughter."

"How long ago?" Nichols climbed back behind the wheel.

"Fifteen minutes, tops." Brad climbed into the passenger seat. "I have no idea where they went."

"We'll find her." Nichols faced him. "Marilu has a tracker. So do you. We couldn't find her before because the one Hoover injected in her overrode the one we put in. I'll have IT see if they can't reinstate hers."

"I have a tracker?" Brad wanted to punch the man. Friend or not, boss or not, the agency had overstepped their bounds. He thought only undercover double agents had trackers. "I want mine destroyed. Consider this my resignation as soon as we rescue Mari and her daughter. I cut

Mari's out of her."

"She has two. One from us, one from them. It's for the protection of every agent. The tracker is effective as long as the person carrying it is alive. That's why it took us so long to locate Marilu. At first, we thought she was dead. When we realized she wasn't, we couldn't block the other transmission." Nichols punched buttons on a phone on the truck's dash, barked orders to reinstate Mari's tracker, then hung up and sped from the driveway. "By the way, we didn't have any more bullet proof vehicles, so try not to get shot.

"Mine and the other vehicle are the only ones we could get to come. We'll follow these other tracks as far as we can. Hopefully by then we'll have a bead on Marilu."

Brad didn't hold out much hope. Instead, he wanted to comb the entire mountain until he found them. "How long?"

"No more than an hour, hopefully." Nichols took a sharp right down a side road.

"And we can trust the man doing the work?"

"I believe so."

Brad stared out the window. Did Hoover know about Mari's GPS? "Where are our trackers?"

"Forearm. If you press hard two inches below the crook of your elbow, you'll feel it."

Brad pressed on what felt like scar tissue. "Can this explode?"

Nichols looked at him as if he'd lost his mind. "We want to keep tabs on our agents, not kill them."

The spot itched. If he'd had the time, Brad would have dug the small disc out of his body and crushed it under his boot. For now, maybe it was better to leave it where it was, in case he went missing or better yet, found Mari. Nichols could save them by their trackers.

The dash phone rang. Nichols lunged for it. "You did? Where? Get us more backup." After hanging up, he turned to Brad. "They got her tracker working. They're close. Other side of the mountain. Ten miles at the most." He flipped open a laptop. A small red dot bleeped from the right of the screen.

The stirrings of hope flooded through Brad. They'd find her. "I'm still resigning."

"I understand. The local police force will be lucky to have you."

"How did you know?"

Nichols shrugged. "It's what all our people do when they leave. After working for us, they can't seem to leave law enforcement altogether."

It's hard to walk away from something that helps protect the innocent. It never occurred to Brad to be anything but a law enforcement officer. With his credentials, he should be able to step right in as a detective.

The trees thickened as they moved closer to where Mari should be. Little snow fell through the thick pines to cover the ground, making travel easier and faster. The closer they got to the blip on Nichols's laptop screen, the quicker Brad's heartbeat. They were closing in.

The sun set, casting the mountain in darkness. Nichols bent forward over the steering wheel. "I don't want to turn on the lights and give us away. Help me watch to make sure we're headed in the right direction."

It wouldn't help any if they ran into a tree or boulder. Brad would go forward on foot if need be, but he liked having the back up of a man with Nichols's experience. "How far behind us is back up?"

"There're two guys in the truck behind us and hopefully a minimum of six more coming. It will take them a couple of hours. They've been on standby on the freeway. No sense having them follow before we knew we could climb to the top with all this ice."

"Too bad we couldn't bring in a helicopter."

"I thought of it, but there's no place to land one." Nichols swerved to miss a large rock. "This is dangerous driving, even for me."

"Don't slow down. Mari's life depends on our haste." Even with the reckless speed Nichols kept, time passed too slow. Brad kept glancing at the flashing red dot on the laptop. As long as it blinked, Mari was safe.

Clouds scurried across the moon, making the night darker. Brad leaned forward, his mouth becoming drier at each tree they passed. Nichols had slowed to twenty miles an hour, still too fast for safety, but too slow for Brad. Any faster was suicide. They couldn't help anyone if they were dead. Please, God, keep her safe until they got there.

"What about Mari's parents?"

"I'm sure they're safely on the way to headquarters. We didn't plan on leaving them at the cabin."

"Good." One less thing for Mari to worry about.

Brad glanced back at the laptop. The dot hadn't moved for several minutes. They were getting closer. Maybe a mile or two.

"I have no idea where Hoover plans on staying up here. Satellite doesn't show any buildings."

"A cave, maybe?"

Nichols shrugged. "Possible, I suppose."

Brad's heart stopped. "The dot isn't blinking. It's gone out."

"What?" Nichols glanced at the computer.

"Watch out!" A tree loomed in front of them. Seconds later, they crashed. The windshield shattered, showering them with glass. Brad's head connected with the dashboard. He drifted into blackness.

CHAPTER TWENTY-TWO

Mari screamed as John cut into her arm. Seconds later, he held a small bloody silver disc, in the palm of his hand.

"Can't let your friends know where we are now, can we?" He dropped the disc on the floorboard and smashed it with the butt of his gun. "I can tell by the bandage showing above the neckline of your shirt that you found the one I put there."

She'd had two GPS signals in her? She cradled her injured arm, wanting nothing more than to kill the man grinning at her. Her mind focused on that one act of violence. She pictured herself putting a gun to his head. The thought scared her to death. Saving Jeanna should be her focus, not revenge.

"Wrap your arm." John tossed her a rag. "You're getting blood on the seat."

"Whose fault is that?" She tied the strip of white cloth around her wound.

His eyes widened in surprise, then he laughed. "You're full of spunk again. I'm going to enjoy breaking you. Get out."

Where were they? Mari slid from the back seat and stared at thick trees in every direction. Was John going to torture and eventually kill them here in the middle of nowhere?

Jeanna ran into Mari's arms. Tears ran down her face. "I heard you scream."

"It's nothing." Ignoring the pain in her arm, she hugged her daughter.

"You're hurt."

"I'm fine."

"Such a touching scene." John shoved them apart. "Too bad there isn't time. Move."

"Where are we going?" Mari glared.

John backhanded her, a ring on his right hand cutting her cheek. "I said move."

"Don't hit her!" Jeanna leaped forward and pounded his chest with both fists until one of the other men wrapped his arms around her waist and lifted her off her feet.

"A spitfire like her mother. This should be fun." He motioned the others ahead and grabbed Mari by the arm. His grip pressed into her knife wound.

She gritted her teeth against the pain, not stopping to wipe the blood from the cut on her face. She wouldn't give him the satisfaction of knowing how much pain she was in.

They traveled a hundred yards farther into the woods. One of the men kicked a pile of leaves away from a trapdoor, then opened it, the hinges squeaking.

No. Not a hole in the ground. Mari's steps faltered. She caught a glimpse of Jeanna's frightened face before her daughter was led down wooden steps. For her, Mari could do this. She could do anything if it meant saving her daughter. She glanced around them, taking note of a large boulder and a tree split from a lightning strike. Hopefully, the two landmarks would help her find a way home.

As John released her, she let her arm hang, dripping blood onto the pristine snow. Hurry, Brad.

John gave her a shove toward the hole. "Hurry up."

With a deep breath, Mari took her first step into the darkness. Her heart pounded in her throat. Thankfully, one of the men ahead held a lantern to light their way.

"Where are we?" Mari asked, staring at the stone walls. Somewhere in the distance water dripped, echoing through the tunnel.

"Old slave quarters. Isn't this place magnificent?" John gave her a push. "These tunnels go all through this area. A stroke of genius on my part in finding them."

"I found them." A young man with straggly hair shoved past.

He looked familiar. Mari studied the back of his head. The mole from the agency. The young IT guy. She'd spotted him through the window when Brad ushered her and her family into the waiting room. The young man just made the list of people Mari wanted to hurt.

Ignoring the blood still trailing down her arm, she followed the leaders into a separate tunnel lined with cell-like rooms. First Jeanna, then Mari was shoved into one. At least they were allowed to be together, and the bare bulb hanging from the ceiling kept the room from total darkness. The door slammed shut, and a key turned in the lock.

A single bed was shoved against one wall. Mari plopped down on it. "Sweetie, I need you to tie this bandage tighter around my arm." It wouldn't do either of them any good if she passed out from blood loss.

"Tell me you have a plan." Jeanna unwrapped the soaked bandage and tossed it in a corner. She slipped off her jacket, then her long-sleeved shirt. Under that she wore a simple white tank top.

"There's a knife in my boot. Use it to cut bandages."

"Won't they notice that?" Jeanna took one corner of the shirt in her mouth and ripped. "This will look more improvised."

"How did you get so smart?"

"I watch a lot of crime shows on TV." Jeanna's grin lit up the room and chased away the dread flooding Mari's heart. With an undershirt that now only reached to the middle of her ribcage, Jeanna quickly redressed and then started wrapping Mari's arm.

Mari grunted as she pulled tight. "Brad will find us."

"I know, and Grandpa will be right there with him."

"Most likely Grandma won't let him out of her sight."

"Then Grandpa will be waiting. There." One final yank on the knot and Jeanna finished her doctoring. "Good thing he taught me how to doctor wounded animals, huh?" She started dabbing another piece of cloth against the cut on Mari's cheek.

"Definitely." Mari laid back on the bed and tried to formulate a plan. John had said a series of tunnels. They had to exit somewhere. Maybe the nearest town? A house long forgotten?

How could she and Jeanna get away? The knife in Mari's boot was no match for several armed men. She'd need to find a way to get one of their guns. She was a trained killer, a professional, she could do this.

~

Brad forced his eyes open. His head pounded in time with his heart. At least it was beating. It had stopped the moment the red dot went black. "Nichols?"

"I'm here. Bruised, but alive. Can't say the same for the truck." The front was smashed bad enough they wouldn't be driving out in the same truck.

"What do we do now?"

"We start searching from her last known location." Nichols fished his cell phone from his pocket and punched in numbers. "Don't tell me there's nothing up here! They aren't camping in tents. Find me their location and get someone here. We've wrecked our vehicle." He hung up and shoved his phone back into his pocket. "Imbecile. Don't worry, Morrison, we'll find them."

He prayed they wouldn't be too late. Where did one start looking when there was an entire mountain to search? "It's getting dark."

"We'll sleep in the truck and start fresh in the morning. There are camping blankets and sleeping bags in the back, plus food and water. We'll be fine." Nichols grinned. "You're getting a black eye to go with the purple lump on your forehead."

"You don't look so pretty yourself." A cut ran across the bridge of the big man's nose, and his lip bled.

Nichols tried to shove his door open. "This isn't going to be easy."

"I'll climb through the front window and try your door from the outside." Using his feet, Brad brushed away the loose shards of glass and pushed out what little was left of the window. They'd be spending a cold night outside.

He crawled out, the wind biting at his face. Hopefully, Nichols had gloves in the back of the truck, too. His fingers were already going numb. One look at the driver's side door told him his boss wouldn't get out that way. The door was wrinkled up like an accordion. "You'll have to get out the window."

"Right. Two hundred and fifty pounds of black man squeezing through a little window. Ain't gonna happen."

"Then you'll sit there like a giant sardine stuffed into a can." Brad surveyed their surroundings. By his calculations, they were approximately half a mile from where Mari's tracker went dead. That didn't mean she'd met with harm. Hoover could have planted another blocker or dug the GPS chip out of her. Either one left Brad and Nichols lost in the woods.

"Does the back door open?" Nichols yelled. "It might be easier for me to get out that way."

Brad tried the back driver's side. Stuck. The passenger side opened with a groan. "You can get out that way." Brad pointed at the small rear window in the truck's cab.

Nichols cursed and twisted in his seat, trying to squeeze his bulk into position. Brad laughed at the sight of the man's rear end suspended in the window. "I wish I had a camera."

"Words like that will get you killed." He fell into the truck bed, and rolled out to the ground. "Start unloading the back. We'll have to bunk down there."

Everything in Brad wanted to keep searching, but with the temperature dropping, he had to agree with Nichols. They'd freeze if they continued on through the night. *Stay strong, Mari. I'm coming.*

He started tossing boxes and bags to the ground, then lay the back seats flat to provide a place to stretch out. Once he'd finished, he spread two sleeping bags and grabbed some Mylar blankets. "What kind of food do we have?"

"Candy bars mostly." Nichols stepped to his side, brushing snow from his pants. "My favorite food. I think there are some Twinkies, too. Maybe some chips and granola bars."

"No wonder you weigh so much." Brad dodged the man's fist. "You can't always blame your size on playing football. College was a long time ago."

"Stuff it, Morrison." Nichols grinned and ripped into a pack of Twinkies. "You eat what you like, and I'll feast on what's really good."

They crawled into the back and shut the back door. Brad stared in the direction Mari had disappeared. While he appreciated his boss's antics to keep his spirits up, worry ate at him like a cancer.

While he watched out the window, he prayed for guidance and safety. He and Nichols could have died in the crash and never made it to Mari's rescue. Taken captive, she never would have known what happened to them. She might have felt abandoned as so many agents did when their positions were compromised and they were left to their own devices. Some died in the field protecting their charges.

He fingered the jump drive in his pocket. While they

could all die protecting the names of so many protectors, he prayed it wouldn't come to that. He wanted a future with Mari and her family.

He slipped into his sleeping bag and crossed his arms behind his head. A packet landed on top of him.

"Aspirin." Nichols flopped onto his back, crowding Brad.

"Thanks." The man's body heat already filled the back of the vehicle. Brad smiled. They wouldn't freeze. He fumbled for a water bottle and downed three of the white tablets before laying back down. Sleep would be slow coming while his mind raced with ways to rescue the woman he loved.

"I can hear your mind racing over here," Nichols said. "You won't be much good to her if you're exhausted."

"I know. Trying to come up with a plan, which is hard, since we don't know where she is."

"We'll come up with our plan on the fly. Won't be the first time."

"True." Brad still liked knowing what was going to happen. Charging in by the seat of the pants wasn't his thing. He liked having a plan A and a plan B with a plan C sketched out in pencil.

Right now, he just wanted Mari safe in his arms. What torment was Hoover putting her through? Using her daughter to keep her in line might work for a while, but Mari was still an agent. She'd take incredible risks to protect her child.

CHAPTER TWENTY-THREE

"Hello? My name is Jeanna. Is anyone there?" Mari woke the next morning to her daughter's voice. "What are you doing?"

"I saw this movie once where this crazy guy had all these women locked in a place just like this. I was wondering whether we were the only ones." Jeanna moved back and perched on the bed beside her.

Mari sat up. "I can't believe I fell asleep." Of course they were the only ones. John wasn't a serial killer, he was a paid assassin. He only went after those he was hired to kill, or people who had wronged him. Like her.

What if he came back and tried to take Jeanna? What if it had happened while she was asleep? It was completely irresponsible of her. But last night, her arms wrapped around her daughter in an attempt to keep them both warm, had been the stuff Mari's dreams were made of.

A tray was pushed through an opening in the bottom of the cell door. Jeanna leaped on it like a starving lion.

"Wait." Mari grabbed her arm. "It could be drugged."

"In the movie, the girls were drugged with a needle." She held a bagel halfway to her mouth.

"This isn't the movies."

"I'm starving."

Mari stared at the food, then nodded. "I'll eat. If I'm not knocked out in fifteen minutes, you're safe."

Jeanna rolled her eyes, but sat back and watched as Mari took a couple of bites of everything on the tray, even sipping the cartons of orange juice.

She didn't put anything past John. Since he knew very well the training Mari had, she suspected him to use drugs to subdue her.

When fifteen minutes passed and she felt fine, she motioned for Jeanna to eat her fill. Then they waited. Being underground, Mari had no concept of time, other than the illumination on her watch, which showed eight a.m. She shrugged off the unease that hung like a cloud over her head at them being underground. Now was not the time for nerves.

How long would John keep them there, alone and wondering what he had planned?

Did he plan on keeping her as some sort of sick trophy, or was he biding his time until he killed them? Mari felt for the knife in her boot. She wouldn't let him harm her daughter.

She laid back on the bed and closed her eyes in prayer. While she wasn't afraid to die, she wasn't ready either. Not now that she'd found her family again, and a man she wanted to spend the rest of her life with. But if God called her home, she prayed He spared her little girl.

Opening her eyes, she stared at the ceiling. There. How could she have missed it? In the corner was a small black camera. John had watched her sleep, watched her test the food. The sick man was playing a game.

She waved and stayed on her back, envisioning ways of making him pay for the last ten years of abuse. Not that she'd act on most of the insane methods of torture she wanted to use. She wasn't that person, may not ever have been the killer she'd woke up thinking she was. The one certainty was that she *would* kill in order to save her daughter.

"Mari, how long is he going to keep us here?" Jeanna sat cross-legged on the floor and shoved the tray away. "Is this some kind of mind game? Kill us out of boredom?"

"I don't know. Come sit next to me." Mari patted the bed. When Jeanna didn't move, she patted it harder.

Jeanna rolled her eyes and sat on the bed.

"Don't look," Mari whispered, "but there is a camera in here. Most likely a microphone, too. We need to dismantle the camera before finding a way to escape. Don't look!" She squeezed Jeanna's thigh.

"The camera isn't pointing at the bucket." Jeanna frowned. "Is that where we're supposed to use the restroom? Gross." She got up and moved to the bucket. After a few minutes, she returned.

"Dirt floor, crumbling bricks, we can dig our way out." She flopped back on the bed, causing Mari to have to turn her head to see her. Smart girl. No lip reading.

"We can use my knife."

"Pretend the food made us sick." Jeanna grinned.

"We make a good team. I'll go first." Mari clutched her stomach and doubled over, moaning, before dashing to the cell's corner. She dug for three minutes, barely making a hole large enough to hold water. The best she could tell, one of the tunnels branching out was on the other side. They'd have to find their way, but first things first.

Pride for her daughter's ingenuity lifted some of the oppression off of Mari's shoulders. If only she could remember everything. If only all of her skills had returned to their full capacity, mental and physical. Mari was the adult. It wasn't Jeanna's job to figure out ways of escaping. It was Mari's. How long until the damage to her mind would heal?

When it was Jeanna's turn, the girl set to work like a rabid badger, doubling the size. Throughout the day, they took turns pretending to be sick and digging. By the time their dinner arrived, the hole was big enough to fit Mari's head. By morning, they should have dug enough to escape their room.

The lights flickered, then went out. Jeanna gasped from where she dug in the corner. Mari checked her watch. Ten p.m. "I guess we have a curfew." She crawled to her daughter's side and helped her dig.

The fact that John had yet to make an appearance told her he must not be in the underground prison. He would never have left her alone for this long. At the least, he would have stood on the other side of the door, making comments through the slit in the door that would mess with her mind. The man was a genius at mental abuse.

Using the dark as coverage, Mari resumed digging. Cool air rushed over her face. They were through. She high-fived Jeanna and laid on her back. Scooting forward, her head broke through the last inch of loose dirt.

A tunnel stretched in both directions. Mari's mouth filled with cotton. They'd have to find their way out in the dark.

~

They'd lost an entire day wandering the woods. With no cell phone reception, Brad and Nichols had no communication from the office.

"This is impossible. There's too much ground to cover." Brad leaned against a tree. Mari could already be dead for all they knew. Without her tracker, they had no guidance. No, he was wrong. He closed his eyes and prayed.

Nichols's phone rang. He answered, the grin on his face widening. "There's a series of tunnels and cells around here. An old slave plantation," he said, shutting off his phone. "I lost the connection before they could give me the coordinates, but they'll text them to me. I need to find another spot where the service is better."

"At least we know what we're looking for." Still a bit

like the proverbial needle in a haystack, but more like a knitting needle now. "There's bound to be a door somewhere." He scanned the area for a hill.

The rumble of an engine reached his ears. "Shh." He turned in a slow circle trying to discern where the sound came from. They had to be close, but sound had a way of carrying on the mountain that could easily have a person heading in the wrong direction. His gut, or maybe it was God, told him to head west.

He motioned for Nichols to follow and set out in the direction he felt led. The underbrush thickened, making travel difficult. Several times he held back a branch to prevent it from slapping his friend in the face. They moved too slowly. With each step, his despair grew. Mari had been a prisoner for almost forty-eight hours. There was no telling the horrors she was being forced to endure.

The moments before the sun made its appearance were the coldest. Brad blew on his hands to warm them through the thin wool gloves he wore. A breeze rattled the branches overhead, and he shivered.

At least with buried slave quarters as her prison, Mari was out of the bitter elements. *If*, that's where John had taken her. It was a mighty big if.

"Hold up." Nichols held his phone over his head and turned in a circle. A small beep signaled a text. "We're right on top of the thing."

Brad groaned. They were so close to rescue, and couldn't be farther from finding the entrance. "Where's backup?" Two men against John's several were odds Brad would face, but would rather not have to.

"On their way. Ten minutes once they find a place to land."

Land? They were coming in by air? Brad whirled. Where? The mountain was dense with trees.

"There's a meadow about a hundred yards east of us, they discovered. We'll meet them there." Nichols scribbled the coordinates on a slip of paper and handed it to Brad.

"You go." Brad shoved the paper into his pocket. "I'm going to continue searching for the entrance."

Nichols narrowed his eyes. "Don't think for a second about going in alone. It's suicide. That's an order."

Brad started to protest. He planned on handing in his official resignation once Mari was safe, but the look on his boss's face told him the man would tie him to a tree if he didn't agree. "Fine."

"I mean it, Morrison. We'll get your girl, but you have to wait for backup." Nichols dashed off in the direction of the meadow as the sounds of a chopper whopped above them.

There wasn't much Brad could do until he found the underground door anyway. Just because the coordinates said he was standing on top of the tunnels, didn't mean the door was in the immediate vicinity. He headed in the opposite direction from the meadow.

A small rise on the horizon spurred him faster. Dead leaves crackled underfoot. He slowed. As much as he yearned to rescue Mari, he'd have no chance if discovered. Stealth was the key. He chose the places to put his feet carefully, freezing when he again heard the sound of a vehicle. Louder this time. He parted a low-lying bush.

A dark Suburban idled next to the hill. Behind the wheel, a man lit a cigarette, while another one leaned against the outside of the vehicle. They must be guarding the entrance.

Brad let the branches fall back into place and sat on his haunches. He needed a plan to get rid of them.

He contemplated the age old trick of a rock thrown into the distance, but that would most likely only lure one away.

Another vehicle entered the area, and John Hoover slid from behind the wheel. He said something to the other two men, then disappeared underground. Brad glanced at his watch. Twelve minutes. Where was his back up?

Moments later, Hoover erupted back outside. "Find her. She can't have gotten far."

Brad grinned. Mari had found a way to escape.

Hoover continued to pace the area, shouting orders and cursing. The man leaning against the truck said something and stepped forward. Hoover drew his gun and put a bullet between the man's eyes, dropping him as effectively as a felled tree. The man behind the wheel spun the vehicle in a circle and sped from the area with the promise of locating their prisoners.

If the man was smart, he'd keep driving and put as much distance between himself and the insane Hoover as possible.

A hand tapped Brad's shoulder. He spun, weapon drawn.

"Hey, glad you listened." Nichols grinned. "I see you found the place."

"Yeah, and it sounds as if Mari and the girl have escaped."

"I hope so. Things are about to get messy." Nichols motioned for the ten men in tactical gear to step forward.

Hoover took one look and dove through the tunnel door. "Get him." Nichols ordered his men to continue forward, and anyone else that isn't one of us."

"Alive, sir?" One of the men asked.

"That is not a priority."

The men raced forward. Seconds later, shots rang out.

CHAPTER TWENTY-FOUR

Mari held up a hand to stop Jeanna and crouched in a dark corner of the tunnel. Shots came from somewhere in the distance. Help had arrived, and Mari had no idea which branch to head down to meet them.

Her breath came in sharp gasps as each tunnel grew darker. They seemed to be heading further underground instead of up. The darkness closed in on her, erasing any sense of direction.

"We should head back," Jeanna said. "We've missed a turn somewhere. When I travel tunnels in my video games, I stay to the right. Always. Eventually, I find my way out."

"It's worth a try." Mari kept her knife gripped in her left hand. With her right against the wall, and Jeanna holding onto the waistband of her pants, she started back in the direction they'd come, keeping the wall always to her right.

Voices echoed, shots thundered, and still she couldn't tell from which direction the sounds came. Her nightmares became a reality. Darkness their only companion.

"I can't see you." Jeanna's voice shook. "I've never been in a place so dark.

Mari hoped to never again be in such a place. "Just keep

a tight grip. I hate tight, dark places."

Her hand touched something slimy, and she almost pulled back. If she did, she was afraid she'd never find the wall again. An irrational fear, with the tunnel being maybe five feet across, but the fear stayed with her. Whatever she touched shifted away, and she bit back a shriek.

Footsteps pounded in their direction. Someone collided with Mari, knocking her off her feet. The person cursed. Mari grappled on the dirt floor as she struggled to her feet. Her fingers came in contact with a handgun. She grasped it and plastered her back to the wall. The man cursed again and thundered away.

So much for courage. "Jeanna?" Mari whispered, finding the wall on her right again.

"I'm here. What happened?"

"Someone is running from our protectors, would be my guess. They're frightened enough not to worry about catching us. Grab hold of me again." Mari stuck the knife back in her boot and transferred the gun to her left hand. The cold steel made her feel safer than she had in hours. Let John come for them now.

The tunnel seemed less dark as they walked. They were coming to the end, but what end? Where would they end up?

She increased her pace, almost running toward the light, and skidded to a halt at the end of a large drain which ran into a river. Across the river was a town.

"How do we get down?" Jeanna released her hold and stepped beside Mari.

"I don't know." What was the drain used for?

Mari turned and studied the dark behind them. Somehow, they'd left the tunnels people had once inhabited. Now they stood on the edge of a culvert long dried that may have once been used for runoff. They were trapped. Either they turned and went back the way they'd come, or they jumped. Neither prospect held any appeal.

She sat on the edge, dangling her legs over. A few

minutes of rest wouldn't hurt. Out of the darkness, she had the presence of mind to think more clearly.

Jeanna sat next to her and slipped her hand in Mari's. "I'm glad I'm going through this with you."

Tears stung Mari's eyes. "Me, too. You're very brave."

"I know you'll find a way out of this. I trust you."

Those words of trust gave Mari hope. She stared at the river thirty feet below as the sound of someone coming came from behind them. "If someone arrives, I want you to jump as far out as you can."

"What will you do?"

"Fend them off for as long as I can."

"I won't go without you." Jeanna's eyes, so like Mari's own, widened and shimmered with tears.

"I know you don't feel as if you have to do what I tell you, but you said you trusted me. Was it the truth?"

Jeanna nodded.

"Then you need to do this for me, please. Without thought, without hesitation, when I say jump, you jump."

"But, Mom..."

Mari cupped her face. "I've waited a long time for you to call me that." A rock rattled behind them, spurring Mari to her feet. She pulled Jeanna up and behind her. As afraid of the dark tunnels as she'd been, Mari now felt a terror sharper than anything before. With nothing behind them but open space and a river, and nothing before them but an unseen assailant, they were as trapped as mice in a cage, and the cat was on the prowl.

Please, God, spare my baby. Mari pointed the Glock toward the tunnel opening, then thought better of them knowing she was armed and held it behind her. What was taking them so long to show their face?

"Marilu?" John sang his taunt. "I've found you. How beautiful you look against the backdrop of the trees. Where will you go now? You'll be dead long before your boyfriend finds his way through the maze."

She squinted, trying to make out his form in the shadows. "Come out where I can see you?"

"No. I want to play a little more. It was quite clever of you to dig your way out right under the nose of the idiots I'd hired to watch you. I should have thought of that. You're smarter than I gave you credit for." A rock rolled from the tunnel opening.

"We can't play properly if you don't come out," Mari said. She whispered to Jeanna to get ready.

"Want to wrestle?" John called.

"I'd love to." Mari braced her feet shoulder width apart, her knees loose. She'd love to get her hands on the guy. All her training, all the memories, came back to her in a rush and almost took her down. Instead, she shoved them aside, choosing to hold onto the memories that taught her to kill. If she took John down, she'd take down the organization. He was the ringleader.

John stepped from the tunnel, keeping his nine-millimeter handgun pointed at her head.

"Jump, Jeanna. Now."

~

Brad broke into the last door in the tunnel of cells. Spotting the hole in the floor, he ducked back out. "What's on the other side of that wall?" He pointed his gun into the face of one of their prisoners."

"More tunnels."

"How do I get there from here?"

The man shrugged. "I was hired to watch the video feed. I have no idea."

Brad expelled a breath through his nose. "Who would know?"

"The guy in the red shirt." The man motioned his head toward a man held against the wall. "He has a map."

"Get it," Brad ordered one of his back up, holstering his weapon. "Now." Each minute he had to wait was one more Mari might not have.

Seconds later, he stood in an intersection in a myriad of underground tunnels, the way lit by a flashlight mounted to the hard hat he wore. Mari could be down any one of them. *Please, God, show me the way.*

A gunshot rang out from somewhere in the distance, the sound echoing from any one of the paths. He could already be too late.

No, he refused to think that way. Mari was smart and resourceful. She'd find a way to get her and her daughter to safety.

The radio on his belt crackled as others searched the rest of the tunnels. With everyone rounded up except for Hoover, closing down the assassination ring was nearing a close. Brad wanted to be the one that brought the leader down, but he'd be satisfied with watching it happen. As long as they got to the man before he got to Mari.

Brad took the right branch and soon found himself at a dead end. It might have once been a pass-through, but now fallen rubble blocked his way. He turned and headed back to the left tunnel.

His radio crackled again. "Sir? Air one here. I have a visual. Woman and suspect in a face-off on the edge of a cliff. The girl jumped."

Brad unhooked his radio. "Do you have a clear shot?"

"Negative. Woman is in the way."

"Hold your fire and keep your visual. What are your coordinates?"

Memorizing the location, Brad ran down the next tunnel. Another dead end. What good were coordinates if he couldn't get there without weaving through a maze? Like a mouse chasing cheese, he dashed up and down the tunnels, his fear for Mari's safety growing with each obstacle.

What did the pilot mean Jeanna had jumped? Was she injured? Dead?

"Morrison, where are you?" Nichols's voice came across the radio.

"I have no idea," Brad answered. "This map is worthless."

"There are markings on the tunnel walls. One of the tunnels isn't actually a tunnel, but drainage. The tunnels would sometimes flood. Mari is in the drainage. I repeat…Mari is in the drainage."

"Where's the drainage?!" Brad crushed the map in his hand. Stupid, worthless piece of paper.

He needed to think systematically and stop rushing along on a wave of emotion. He smoothed the map back out, noting how the tunnels formed a wagon wheel. Wheels had an even number of spokes, right? He counted the ones on the paper. Thirteen. Which one was the drainage?

He held the paper against the wall and studied the ink drawing. One of the spokes seemed out of place. Rather than a uniform distance from the others, it was, instead, in the center of two. Brad shined his light along the wall. This tunnel had a triangle carved into the wall. He needed to make it to the tunnel with a circle. The next one should be the drainage.

He dashed off, stopping at each entrance long enough to find the carving on the wall before rushing away. How much time had passed? Was Mari still facing Hoover, or had the man finally finished her off? Brad's footsteps pounded on the dirt floor, his breathing filled the narrow spaces, erasing all other sounds.

There! The circle. He whirled and sprinted down the next tunnel toward a small circle of light. It was his worst nightmare. One where he ran and ran toward the light, never reaching the end of darkness.

He could finally make out Hoover outlined by the sun. Past him, stood Mari on the edge of a cliff, one hand held behind her back. Brad pulled his weapon and crept closer.

"Come now, darling," Hoover said. "You're my wife. Is this any way to act toward the grieving husband?"

"We weren't really married." Mari glanced over her

shoulder.

"Oh, but we were. See, in my own way, I fell in love with you." Hoover took another step closer. "Your marriage to Jack Hutchins might have been a fake, but I can assure you that ours is very much real."

"Then I want a divorce."

Hoover laughed, aiming his gun at her heart. "I'm afraid that isn't possible. I believe marriage is forever. Until death do us part. You know the routine."

"Then consider it over." Mari swung her arm up. In her hand, she clutched a Glock.

Two shots rang out simultaneously, one bringing Hoover to his knees, the other sending Mari over the cliff. Brad yelled and rushed forward.

Hoover shot out a foot and tripped him, sending Brad face first into the dirt and decaying leaves. Brad turned, squeezing his trigger. His bullet caught Hoover between the eyes. Mari's shot had caught the man in the stomach, covering his once-pristine white snow coat with blood. "Consider yourself no longer married."

Brad crawled to the edge of the cliff. Mari's head broke the surface of the river as the current swept her away.

CHAPTER TWENTY-FIVE

Mari gasped as she came up for air. John's bullet had grazed her shoulder as she'd turned to jump. The contact with the river below hurt more than the burn from his shot. "Jeanna!"

She'd never thought to ask her daughter whether she could swim. If not, the river's swift current would have pulled her under in seconds. Mari fought to stay afloat, taking deep gulps of air each time her head broke the water's surface.

"Mom!"

Mari glanced toward the shoreline. Jeanna leaped over rocks and fallen logs in an attempt to keep up with Mari's mad water ride. With her daughter in sight, Mari fought the current to the smoother water close to the shore. Hooking her arms around a limb hanging low over the water's edge, she fought to catch her breath while the river did everything in its power to pull her free.

"Stay back, honey." The limb dipped lower, submerging Mari. She pulled herself back up and, using the branch, pulled herself to the shore. Once on the wet soil, she flopped over to her back and gasped like a fish. She'd lost her weapon going into the water and prayed she wouldn't need it.

Jeanna leaned over her, eyes wide, a gash along her cheek was bleeding. "You made it." Her teeth shined white under the mud covering most of her face.

"I did." Mari struggled to sit up. "I'm not sorry to say that I doubt John Hoover will be joining us." Not since she'd caught a glimpse of Brad just as she went over the cliff. If her bullet hadn't finished off John, then Brad most certainly would have.

It bothered her that she'd been instrumental in taking a life, but the man wouldn't have had the same qualms about ending her's or Jeanna's. If John was telling the truth, Mari was now a widow. She flopped back and laughed. The sound boomed through the trees and startled birds from their roosts.

"What do we do now?" Jeanna sat cross-legged beside her, her arms wrapped around her middle as she shivered.

"We can follow the river to civilization or wait until someone finds us." Mari stopped laughing and cupped her daughter's face. "I'm tired. I vote we wait a while."

"It's cold, and you're bleeding."

"It is cold, but I'll be fine. It's just a graze." Mari held out her arms. Jeanna laid down beside her and cuddled close, adding her warmth to Mari's.

As tired as she was, they couldn't stay long, but rest sounded so wonderful. She'd done it. Protected her daughter and gotten them free from the clutches of a madman. Brad had come. He'd find them soon. She closed her eyes and slept.

"Mari!"

She woke to Brad barging through the trees. The sun sat low on the horizon. He slid to a stop beside her and gathered her into his arms. "I thought I'd lost you. When I saw you go over that cliff—"

"All part of my escape plan." She smiled at the man she loved so much. Reaching up, she smoothed away the worry

171

line from between his eyes. "Thank you for coming."

"I couldn't think of anything else. It took us all day to round up these guys and comb the river's edge to find you." He helped her to her feet. "Let's get the two of you out of here."

"That's the best thing I've heard all day." Mari held out her other hand to Jeanna. "Ready to go home?"

"Past ready." Jeanna grinned.

Together, the three of them made their way to where Nichols and six other men in tactical gear huddled around a van full of the very men who had held Mari and Jeanna captive. "Where's John?"

"Inside, wrapped in a cozy black bag." Nichols grabbed her to his massive chest. "Glad to see you, girl. Still thinking of resigning?"

"Definitely."

"I'm joining her," Brad said. "I plan on giving this woman the white picket fence, kids, and a dog. Anything she wants."

Mari turned to face him. Joy leaped inside of her. "Shouldn't you ask me first?"

"Ask you what?" His brow furrowed.

"Whether I'll marry you." She tried to look serious, and failed. Nothing could keep her happiness from exploding across her face in the form of a grin.

Brad dropped to one knee and took her hand in his. "This might not be the place, but I don't want to waste another second. Will you marry me, Marilu Hastings Hoover?"

"As soon as we get off this mountain."

He got to his feet and pulled her close, claiming her lips with his own. The men behind them cheered. Jeanna dashed forward and wrapped her arms around them both.

The End

Continuing reading for the first chapter of Captured Innocence

CAPTURED INNOCENCE

CHAPTER ONE

The night breeze carried whispers of her name.

Footsteps sounded behind her.

A chill coursed down her spine, prickling her skin with goose bumps.

Jocelyn Nielson pulled her ratty brown sweater tighter across her chest and risked another peek over her shoulder. She paused, and the echoing footfalls stopped. Maybe she'd imagined the sound in the first place. She didn't see anyone out of the ordinary. No one paid her undue attention. She raised a hand to her throat and took a deep breath. Her gaze swept the sidewalk.

A few older women window shopped, pointing, and gasping at prices. A young man stood on the corner to hail a taxi. His shrill whistle pierced Jo's ears. A group of teenage girls giggled as they ambled along the sidewalk and stopped under a street lamp. They looked in compact mirrors or punched numbers into their brightly colored cell phones.

Jo examined their low rise jeans and designer tops.

She smoothed the skirt of the full dress she wore and plucked at the sleeve of her button up sweater. Twenty-five, and she dressed like an old maid. She sighed. Someday—when she felt safe. Safe enough to believe her ex-husband wouldn't find her, then, she'd go on with her life. She'd wear pretty clothes again.

Quickening her pace, she stopped beneath the street lamp and checked her watch. Eight o'clock! She was late picking up Alex from the babysitter. Again. Why had she covered the other waitress's shift? She pressed her hand against her forehead. *Because I need the money, that's why.*

She darted to merge with the group of teenagers who assessed her with scornful looks and turned their attention back to each other. She walked with them for two blocks, marveling at their ability to chatter so animatedly and ignore her presence. When had she ever been so carefree?

A few minutes later, she left them and stopped in front of a dark alley. A short cut, it would shave fifteen minutes off her walk. She took another glance at her watch then scanned the sidewalk behind her. Her ears strained to hear sounds of pursuit. Nothing.

Taking a shaky breath, she stepped into the dimness of the alley. Every horror movie of stupid heroines ran through her mind. She shrugged. Making up the time she'd lost was more important. She couldn't afford to find another babysitter, and she'd been warned many times about being late.

The night wind tore down the alley. Jo's long hair whipped from her pony tail and around her face, obscuring her vision.

An aluminum can rattled.

Her heart leapt into her throat.

175

She froze, then spun and shoved her hair from her face. Her eyes scanned the darkness behind her.

The streetlight cast a yellow glow over the entrance to the alley. The figure of a man stood in silhouette, legs parted, hands held loosely at his sides. A trench coat flapped around his knees.

She gasped and ran away from the light. Away from the stranger. Her breath rasped, and her heart pounded against her ribcage. The sound of her own frantic footsteps masked those of any would-be assailant.

A brick wall loomed.

Panic rioted through her as she whirled, searching for a place to hide. She ducked behind a dumpster and risked another glance down the alley. Her blood pounded in her ears.

There was no one to be seen. No sound of stalking feet. No cans rattled. Only the wind blew and whistled across several open lids of other dumpsters lining the alley.

Jo turned toward a scurrying sound. Red beady eyes stared at her from under a cardboard box. She screamed. A rat darted from its hiding place.

She rose, poised for flight like a wild animal who'd caught an unfamiliar scent. Her gaze darted from one corner of the alley to another, anxiously trying to find a way around the brick obstacle.

"Jocelyn." A soft, sinister voice sliced through her quickly unraveling nerves. It couldn't be him, could it? There could be no way he knew where she'd run to.

A cat leapt from the dumpster, and the lid rattled like distant thunder. Jo collapsed back onto a pile of garbage bags someone had neglected to dispose of.

"Jocelyn." The voice came again. Clearer. Louder.

She scrambled to her feet. Her shoes slipped on the rotten vegetable matter that oozed from the ripped bags.

A rancid smell assaulted her. Her hand plunged into a gooey substance. She shook it clean. A sob caught in her throat.

"What do you want with me?" Her voice came out as a hoarse whisper. "Please leave me alone."

The rising wind tangled her skirt around her legs. With one hand on her sweater, she tried holding down her skirt with the other.

The man seemed to have disappeared. He no longer called her name in that eerie sing-song way. His shadow no longer stretched down the alley.

She spotted a small gate to the right of the brick wall. She eased toward it, straining to listen for footsteps in pursuit. She glanced over her shoulder every few feet.

A bang, a crash, and a thud somewhere in the dark spurred her faster. She ran and resisted the urge to look back. Reaching the end of the alley, she turned right. The two blocks to her apartment building seemed like two miles.

Her shoes tapped out a beat as she half-ran, half-walked. Several people glanced her way, and she ducked her head to avoid their faces. Tears poured down her cheeks, and she swiped them away.

One man reached out to stop her. "Are you all right?"

Jo halted and glanced up. Blue eyes locked with hers. The man stepped toward her. She squeaked in alarm and darted away from him.

"Wait," he called after her. "Let me help you."

Jo glanced back. Her eyes were drawn to the tall man, lean, with massive shoulders. A scream bottled in her throat. She sprinted around the corner and burst through the gate to the fence circling her apartment building.

She put a hand to her chest. She wheezed like a squeaky screen door. Jo patted her pockets for her inhaler. Stupid! She'd left it upstairs in her apartment.

Risking one more look down the street, she rammed her key into the lock of the security door. Slipping inside, she closed the door and leaned against it, concentrating on regulating her breathing. Precious seconds ticked by before her breathing slowed. "I'm a fool," she whispered to herself. *Taking the alley as a shortcut.*

Taking the stairs two at a time, she used the railing to pull herself along, and came to a noisy stop outside her babysitter's apartment door. She took a deep breath. She still wheezed, but with less pain, and rang the bell.

"You're late." Mrs. Leonard frowned at her, her severe face drawn into disapproving wrinkles.

"I'm so sorry. I was held up at work." Jo transferred her attention to her five-year-old son, who stood next to the babysitter. "Hey, baby. Sorry I'm late."

Alex gazed up at her with dark brown eyes, so like her own. They never failed to brighten Jo's day, no matter how hectic it had been. "That's okay, Mommy. You're here now."

Jo bent and kissed her son's cheek. "You're so sweet. I don't deserve you."

"You're squeaking," Alex said.

"I ran. Didn't want to be too late picking up my little man, did I? I'm okay."

Mrs. Leonard continued to stare down her nose at them, as if in silent agreement about Jo's statement of her unworthiness. Jo took a deep breath and straightened to meet the older woman's eyes.

"I told you what I would have to do if you were late again."

"I understand, Mrs. Leonard, but…"

"You are not setting a good example for your son, Ms. Kingsley." Mrs. Leonard folded her thin arms across her flat chest. "Punctuality is a worthy trait."

"Please." Jo hated the pleading tone that crept into her voice. "Alex is such a good boy. You've said he doesn't cause you a bit of trouble."

"That's beside the point. This happens too often. My time is valuable. I have a life besides caring for your son."

Jo's heart skipped a beat. "I'll pay you extra. I can't afford to lose you or my job. You have to realize I would never abandon my son." She squared her shoulders. "I'll pay you an extra ten dollars a week to cover any evenings I run late." *How will I ever afford it?*

Mrs. Leonard sniffed. "I don't like it. Being consistently late isn't good parenting."

Alex grasped the older woman's hand. "Please." He raised his eyes to hers and smiled.

A smile twitched at the corner of the other woman's mouth. "All right, Alex."

Jo relaxed her shoulders and took her son's hand. At least the woman had a soft spot for her son. "Let's get you to bed, sir."

Her son chattered non-stop as they climbed the two flights of stairs to their small one bedroom apartment. He regaled Jo with tales of what he'd learned in Kindergarten before the bus dropped him into Mrs. Leonard's care.

"What did you do with Mrs. Leonard today?"

Alex frowned. "She makes me do my homework

first thing. Then I can watch cartoons. Sometimes I help her fold laundry."

"Laundry? Really?" Jo chuckled and unlocked the door to their apartment. She pulled the chain on the overhead light and grimaced as cockroaches scurried for cover. The landlord had promised her he would spray.

She spotted her inhaler on the kitchen table and grabbed it to take two puffs of the medication. She felt her bronchial tubes relax. "Come on, Alex. We have to see Mr. Every."

"I don't like him," Alex said. "He's mean. Like a stranger."

She looked at her son. "I agree, but we've got to be polite. Okay?"

"Okay." The little boy slid his hand into hers.

With a firm grasp on Alex's hand, Jo led the way down the three flights of steps to the first floor. She rapped on the door labeled 'Manager', then buttoned her sweater to the top button, covering the thin white blouse beneath.

"Jo." The man stunk of body sweat and beer. He wore faded black slacks and a stained, sleeveless tee shirt that strained to cover a large paunch, a ludicrous addition to his gaunt frame.

Jo wrinkled her nose and stepped back. "Mr. Every, there are still cockroaches in my apartment. You promised you would take care of them." She averted her eyes from the way he'd combed thinning hair slicked over to one side of his head in a vain attempt not to appear bald.

"Now, Jo." He stepped aside and flung an arm wide, inviting her inside. "Let's talk about this inside."

"There's nothing to talk about. You promised. A man's word should be concrete."

His eyes narrowed, and his gaze ran slowly over her body. Jo clenched her fists at her side and struggled to remain where she stood and not shrink back. Her flesh crawled, and she mentally counted her loose change, estimating whether she had enough for a bath. The apartments shared several bathrooms, charging a dollar for each short shower.

"Jo, things could be so much easier for you if you'd only let me…"

"Besides the bugs, things are fine as they are."

His face flushed. "I could give you so many more things. A woman with your beauty should have the finer…"

"No, thank you." *I've had it before.*

A muscle twitched near Mr. Every's eye. "There's a charge for me taking care of bugs for you. Maybe you need to clean your apartment. I haven't had complaints from the other tenants."

"A charge? Clean my apartment? Fumigating should be one of your duties as apartment manager." Alex yelped, and Jo loosened her hold on his hand. She mouthed "sorry" and turned back to the scowling man.

"That's the way of it, unless we could come to an agreement of some sort." He leered at her.

"So, unless I give you special privileges, you won't take care of my problem. Is that right?"

"Pretty much." He spit on the floor at her feet.

Jo spun and dragged Alex with her. "Fine. I'll take care of it myself."

She stomped up the stairs, jerking her son along beside her. "I'm sorry, sweetheart. I've got to get away from that man before I do something bad." Her voice shook, and tears prickled behind her eyelids.

"Are you going to cry, Mommy? Sometimes crying helps." Her son patted her arm.

She blinked back the tears and gave him a shaky smile. "How did you get so smart?"

"I'll kill the bugs for you," Alex said. "Smash them and throw them out the window."

Jo laughed. "There're way too many. And the window is painted shut."

"I can kill some of them. I'll toss them in the garbage. That's better than nothing. Mrs. Leonard stepped on one today. I hardly never see them in her place."

"It's hardly ever, and I'm sure you don't see bugs anywhere near her. They wouldn't dare." She opened their apartment door and tousled the boy's hair as she let him precede her. "Why don't you go on a bug hunt while I fix us something for dinner?"

She had a difficult time preparing chicken noodle soup and sandwiches as Alex flicked the light on and off in his hunt for the distasteful bugs. She laughed when he yelled triumphantly each time his shoe made contact.

He ran into the kitchen, shoe held high as he chased one of the insects. Jo jumped and shrank back against the wall, cringing at the crunch of the shoe on the bug's armor.

She waited for the light to come back on before setting the bowls on the small, scarred dining table. The wooden top had once been varnished a honey oak color. Now it was faded. Two plastic lawn chairs served as their seats.

She looked around the room they'd lived in for the past few months, at the faded, peeling, striped wallpaper. She didn't have a clue what its original color had been, but now it was different shades of grey. She took in the chipped paint on the metal kitchen cabinets—the hot plate that served as their stove.

Her son happily ate the meager dinner she'd prepared and the tears threatened again. They lived on soup and sandwiches or macaroni and cheese. Once in a while she'd bring home something from work. A real treat.

Alex was smaller than most of the children in his class. Life should have been different. It *had* been different, until she'd married *him*. Not perfect, but not this either. She shook her head, shying from the memory. As if by thinking about him, she would alert him to their presence.

Jo lifted the spoon to her mouth and smiled around the utensil at her son. Alex beamed back at her, and suddenly, the glamorous life she'd lived before her son's birth didn't seem so important.

She sighed and finished her meal, then removed the dinner dishes from the table. "Brush your teeth and get in bed. I'll be there in a minute."

The rhythmic movement of her hands as she washed dishes, and the lavender scent of the dish soap soothed her, erasing the fear and stress of the day.

Alex spit into the sink beside her, and she frowned. They couldn't even afford an apartment with a separate bathroom and even with rent as cheap as she paid, she didn't see improvements in the near future. It was like living in the 1900s. What kind of people spit into their kitchen sink? *People in our circumstances, that's who.* She replaced the dishes on the shelf that served as their dish cabinet and turned to usher Alex into bed.

She tucked him into the single bed in the small eight-by-ten foot bedroom and smoothed the dark hair back from his forehead. "You need a haircut." Jo planted a kiss on his forehead. "I'm off work tomorrow. How would you like to play hooky from school?"

"Can we go to the zoo?" A look of hopefulness, mixed with the fear of disappointment, shadowed his face.

Jo wracked her brain for ways of cutting costs in order to be able to afford the outing. They'd manage. Somehow. Alex had too little fun in his life. "You bet."

"Night, Mommy." Alex closed his eyes and turned on his side.

"Goodnight, sweetheart." Jo gave him another glance before closing the door. Her heart lay heavy in her chest as she prepared her bed on the lumpy sofa.

She thought again of her husband, his hard-handed, controlling ways, and punched her pillow into a shape for her head. *God, where are you?*

She sniffed and lay on her back to shift her weight on broken springs. *I've run for three years. Hoping...praying for a place to raise my son in safety.* A place where his father's long arm and wealth couldn't reach them. *Help us. Please, God.*

*

After the crying woman bolted into the apartment building, Conley headed back the way the woman had come. H stopped in front of the dark alley and listened, then ventured toward the opposite end.

Nothing moved. No cat or rat. No dogs howled. A gust of wind rattled the pages of a newspaper, and he swung his head around. Not seeing anyone, he continued his search. Here is where she'd hidden behind the dumpster. A few more feet and he found the torn garbage bags where she'd fallen.

Laughter rang out from the street. He ducked into an

alcove.

A man, staggering drunk, and his female companion entered the alley, tottering and giggling. They kissed and groped each other as they fell to the ground, unmindful of the filth and wet.

Conley stuffed his hands into the pockets of his jeans and leaned back, bracing his right leg against the brick wall. He'd acted on a hunch anyway. He doubted she'd be carrying a clue to her real identity.

Ten minutes later, the drunken pair left the alley, leaning on each other for support. The woman laughed shrilly after she tripped and almost fell.

With one last glance around, Conley headed back toward the apartment building. His cowboy boots clomped against the almost deserted street.

He watched the light flicker on in the third floor apartment. The shape of a woman passed by the window. A child's form joined hers, and the woman pulled the child close for a hug. The picture warmed him, despite the chill in the air. He'd been hired to do a job, he no longer had the heart for.

Forty-five minutes later, the apartment light turned off. Conley pushed the button on his watch, illuminating the face. Ten o'clock. He leaned against the wall under a large oak tree and continued to watch the window. His neck ached from peering upward. He waited an hour to see whether the light would come back on. It didn't.

The wind blew colder, and he shoved his hands into the pockets of his jeans, hunching forward. Too bad he hadn't brought a jacket. Long strides carried him quickly down the street. How would he tell the woman who he really was without her running again?

Check out Captured Innocence by scanning this code

ABOUT THE AUTHOR

Website at www.cynthiahickey.com

Also www.forgetmenotromances.com

Multi-published and Amazon Best-Selling author Cynthia Hickey had three cozy mysteries and two novellas published through Barbour Publishing. Her first mystery, Fudge-Laced Felonies, won first place in the inspirational category of the Great Expectations contest in 2007. Her third cozy, Chocolate-Covered Crime, received a four-star review from Romantic Times. All three cozies have been re-released as ebooks through the MacGregor Literary Agency, along with a new cozy series, all of which stay in the top 50 of Amazon's ebooks for their genre. She had several historical romances release through Harlequin's Heartsong Presents, and has sold close to a million copies of her works since 2013. She has taught a Continuing Education class at the 2015 American Christian Fiction Writers conference. You can find her on FB, twitter, and Goodreads, and is a contributor to Cozy Mystery Magazine blog and Suspense Sisters blog. She and her husband run the small press, Forget Me Not Romances, which includes some of the CBA's best well-known authors. She lives in Arizona with her husband, one of their seven children, two dogs, two cats, three box turtles, and two Sulcata tortoises. She has seven grandchildren who keep her busy and tell everyone they know that "Nana is a writer".